'Roger!'

The children's cries   ening. As usual they crowded ar   him, and he spoke to them all, teasing them, ruffling their hair and making them laugh.

Jennifer was wheeling away the bin when a shiver ran down her spine as she felt the doctor's large firm arm across her shoulders. She swung around and saw, with mixed feelings, that his other arm was on Debbie, who was smiling completely unselfconsciously.

'And how are my two favourite nurses?' he asked.

'Blooming,' Debbie replied. 'I'm trying to persuade Jennifer to come to Firth's party on Saturday. Lend your weight to my persuasions or she'll be stuck at home thinking nobody loves her.'

He looked down at Jennifer, his dark brown eyes gently caressing. 'We can't have that, can we, Debbie?'

But Debbie had gone to attend to one of the babies. Seeing that they were alone, he said, 'Do come.' And Jennifer felt the increased pressure of his hand.

She said too brightly, 'I'll have to see if my boy-friend is free.'

Roger looked at her for what seemed a long time but could only have been a couple of seconds. She felt the blood rushing to her cheeks and cursed herself for blushing. It always made her feel so embarrassed. It was no use telling herself that it was her body pumping out adrenalin which made some blood vessels relax and others contract, because that piece of knowledge learned at early lectures didn't help at all . . .

Rhona Trezise was brought up in Cornwall. On her marriage to an architect she moved to London where they had a son and daughter. In 1967 she started writing short stories for women's magazines and the BBC, as well as picture scripts for teenagers and articles for educational journals. Having spent some time as a patient in various hospitals, she was so impressed by the loving care and charm of the nurses and doctors that she was prompted to weave romances around them. She obtains her medical information from many friends in the profession and from textbooks and medical journals.

The Children's Doctor is Rhona Trezise's eighth Doctor Nurse Romance. Recent titles include *Nurse Hannah*, *Suzanne and the Doctor* and *Nurse in the Sun*.

THE CHILDREN'S DOCTOR

BY

RHONA TREZISE

MILLS & BOON LIMITED
ETON HOUSE 18–24 PARADISE ROAD
RICHMOND SURREY TW9 1SR

First published in Great Britain 1987 by Mills & Boon Limited

© Rhona Trezise 1987

Australian copyright 1987 Philippine copyright 1987

ISBN 0 263 75878 8

Set in 11 on 12½ pt Linotron Times
03–1087–42,500

Photoset by Rowland Phototypesetting Limited Bury St Edmunds, Suffolk Made and printed in Great Britain by William Collins Sons & Co Limited, Glasgow

CHAPTER ONE

HENLEY was in holiday mood. Men and women in gay summer clothes strolled beside the river watching the pleasure launches and rowing-boats on the sun-dappled water. Jennifer Langford, seated in the striped kiosk, rested her pretty heart-shaped face on her hands and gazed into space, feeling solitary and apart. The smell of the ice-cream in the kiosk was overpowering and brought vividly to mind the scent of the roses and lilies of the valley that had made up her bridal bouquet. Inevitably her thoughts moved on to her wedding-gown in crisp ivory taffeta wreathed with a veil of Honiton lace. It was as alien to her as if she had merely tried it on in a boutique; she had not worn it long enough to feel that it belonged to her. But she remembered the expression on her father's face of pleased pride as he stood looking like a stranger in a hired morning suit and watched her coming down the stairs to join him. He had told her in a gruff voice that she looked beautiful and had given her a rare, embarrassed kiss.

The picture disintegrated as a group of noisy teenagers demanded cornets and wafers and laughed and joked amongst themselves. She

5

loathed the stickiness and the increased odour as she ladled out the ice-cream, but even more she hated the silence when the youngsters moved away. In her renewed solitude her thoughts returned to that dreadful day. During the week running up to it her friends and colleagues had said they would pray for a fine day, and their prayers had been answered, for it was warm and sunny. The fifteenth-century church set amidst cypress trees made a charming background for the bridesmaids as they waited beside the door in their apricot nylon dresses and carrying posies of multi-coloured rosebuds. It made a picture that was imprinted on Jennifer's mind, and was one she would never forget.

As her wedding car reached the entrance the chief bridesmaid, clutching her skirt, ran down to speak to her.

'Simon and Barry haven't arrived yet,' she said breathlessly.

Jennifer's father leaned forward and spoke to the driver, then glanced at Jennifer and said, 'He's going to drive around the block again. Simon's car must have broken down.'

She had felt sorry for Simon at the time, for he was a perfectionist and punctual to a fault, and she knew how worried he would be. It was not until they had arrived at the church for the third time that a knot of anxiety that had been slowly forming inside her tightened, and the aura of embarrassment in the car was overwhelming. By then it came as a terrible shock but no surprise when somebody arrived to tell them that Simon had changed his mind and that the wedding was off.

'Two wafers, please, large ones.'

Jennifer looked at the customer with bemused blue eyes and automatically prepared the order.

'Lovely day, isn't it?' the woman said.

Jennifer smiled and agreed, then went back to her thoughts.

It must have been dreadfully difficult for her parents to decide what to do next, but the reception was held as arranged, as a number of the guests had travelled some distance and would be expecting a meal. She shuddered as she remembered how her mother had tried to persuade her to attend the reception; she said it would be better to face everybody right away and get it over and done with, and Jennifer supposed that made sense, but she couldn't do it. Instead she went home and her brother, on special leave from the Army, went with her. He made some strong sweet tea and wrapped a towel around her dress to protect it.

'I should get changed when you've drunk that,' he advised gruffly.

She held the cup with shaking hands. 'Why would he do this to me, Ian? Why?' she asked over and over again.

'Got cold feet, I s'pose—some blokes do. He'll feel different in a day or two, you'll see. Get his second wind.'

She knew Ian was trying to comfort her, but his suggestion was obscene. She never wanted to see Simon again, or the guests, who were largely made up of the staff at the Exmouth hospital where they both worked, he as a dental surgeon, she as a staff nurse. She could never go back there and face them all again. It had been like a lifeline when her Aunt Marian had suggested that she went back with her to Henley-on-Thames. There were just the two of them, herself and Bernard, her son, so having Jennifer would present no problem and she was welcome to stay for as long as she wished.

'A small cornet, please.'

Jennifer prepared it and waited while the woman searched for her purse. She watched with uninterest a small boy hopping inexpertly along the river bank, the sunlight turning his golden hair silver.

In the same instant that he disappeared from view, Jennifer flung down the cornet and raced across the road. As she feared, he had fallen into the river. She reached out to grab him, but the fast-flowing water carried him away, and she over-balanced and fell in. She knew she must reach him before he was swept into mid-stream by the current, because she knew that not far downstream was a treacherous weir. Kicking off her sandals, she swam with all her strength and slowly gained on him. She reached for him thankfully, but he struggled and slipped from her grasp. Breathless and impeded by her clothing, she nevertheless managed to grab him a second time and was able to swim with him towards the bank, but she knew she would not be able to drag them both to safety. Some youths were laughing and fooling about a small distance away. She called to them, but they were making too much noise to hear her and continued their play, pretending to push one another over the edge.

'Help, help!' she called as loudly as she could.

They saw her then and ran along the bank, holding on to each other as they reached down, but it was difficult for them to get a grip on the child. They pulled and Jennifer tried to lift, and at last he was safely hoisted up. Then they helped Jennifer to climb out. She saw with relief that the little boy was coughing up water and then began to cry lustily. Although she was shivering with cold and fear she held him close to reassure him, while the boys stood around watching, enjoying the unexpected excitement.

'Where you got to go?' they asked.

She pointed to the kiosk. 'Over there.'

'Okay, I'll carry the nipper,' a boy with green and purple hair offered.

Jennifer thanked him and picked her way carefully over the rough ground, as she shivered and trembled.

The woman she had been about to serve was leaning ashen-faced against the kiosk.

'Thank God—oh, thank God!' she breathed, hugging the crying child. 'You're back with Granny now, Brian.' She looked anxiously at Jennifer. 'Is he all right?'

'He's fine,' Jennifer said casually in a desire to play down the incident. 'But it would be a good idea to get him into a hot bath, he's probably a bit shocked.' She took another look at him. 'Be sure and call your doctor if you're worried about him.'

The woman nodded. 'My husband is a doctor. Can I take you somewhere?'

Jennifer's benefactor with the multi-coloured hair said, 'She ain't got no shoes.'

'Oh dear, you lost them in the river? Then I must drive you to your home. Have you far to go?'

'No, but I could do with the lift,' said Jennifer, then turning to the boys thanked them again. 'Can I give you some ice-cream before I go?'

They stood around expectantly while she made the biggest wafers and cornets she could. She fetched a towel from a hook, then locked up the kiosk. For once visitors would have to buy their ice-cream elsewhere.

She turned to the woman. 'We need to get Brian out of his wet clothes. Have you anything else he could put on?'

'There's a rug in the car—that would do, wouldn't it?'

Jennifer rubbed him briskly with the towel, talking comfortingly to him as she removed his clothes and wrapped him tightly in the rug. Then she dabbed her face and arms and legs and sat in the car beside him.

'I can never thank you enough,' the woman said as she started up the engine. 'This is the first time I've had my grandson to stay. How could I ever have faced my son if anything—if you hadn't been there to save him? I must introduce myself. I'm Mrs Constable, and you are—?'

'Jennifer Langford.' She turned to Brian. 'You're okay, aren't you? I expect we're both going to enjoy a nice hot bath, though, aren't we?'

'Are you a student?' Mrs Constable asked.

'A student?'

'I'm sorry, I just thought—working in the kiosk was probably a holiday job.'

'Well, yes, it's only temporary. I'm really a nurse, but—well, I'm between hospitals at the moment.'

'A nurse? So which hospital are you going to? Our local?'

Jennifer shook her head. 'I'm afraid I haven't been offered anything yet.'

'Oh dear, I know it can be difficult these days. It's the same with everything.' After a moment Mrs Constable said thoughtfully, 'I wonder if my husband could help? Would you like me to have a word with him?'

Jennifer felt a jolt of dismay; she hadn't yet allowed herself to think seriously about the future.

But sooner or later she would have to do so.

'That would be very kind of you,' she replied politely.

'Not at all, it's the very least I can do. Now, let me see. When would be a good time.' Mrs Constable thought for a moment. 'Would Sunday suit you? I'm having a few friends to lunch if you would care to join us? My husband will be home then, but I can never be sure during the week. You could have a chat with him which might be of use.'

The invitation was so unexpected that Jennifer wanted to play for time.

'I'm living in the next road at the moment—the fifth house on the left-hand side.' She waited until Mrs Constable stopped outside her aunt's small Georgian house before replying to the invitation.

'Well, thank you, I should like to join you on Sunday,' she said at last.

'Splendid. I'll give you my card. Shall we say twelve-thirty? And thank you again.' Mrs Constable looked around at Brian, who had started whimpering. 'Please don't start crying now,' she implored.

Jennifer waited until the car was out of sight before reading the card in her hand. Mrs James Constable, The Willows, Henley-on-Thames. There was also a telephone number and a Harley Street address in the bottom corner. This seemed promising, Jennifer decided, but not half as attractive as the prospect of taking off her wet clothes and getting into a hot bath.

As she unlocked the front door she was hoping her aunt would be out. But a sweet-faced woman emerged from a back room and looked out anxiously.

'Oh, it's Jennifer! You're back early—I wondered who it could be. You startled me.' She panted and pressed her hand to her heart to prove her point.

'I'm sorry, Aunt Marian.'

Her aunt moved closer and put out a hand to discover whether her eyes were deceiving her.

'You're wet—soaking!' She glanced down at her feet. 'And where are your shoes? What's happened?'

'That's a good question,' said Jennifer, making for the stairs.

'What *have* you been up to? You're making the carpet wet!'

'Yes, I'm sorry, I mustn't stand here. I'll have a bath and then tell you all about it.' She started up the stairs.

'A bath? Did you say a bath? Oh dear, then I must turn on the immersion heater or Bernard will be angry if the water isn't hot when he gets in. You'd better not be long.'

Jennifer mounted the stairs two at a time. She had an uncharitable longing to shove Bernard into a bath of ice-cold water—everything in this house revolved around him, his likes and dislikes, for at thirty-six he was still his mother's darling.

She went into the bathroom and turned on the water, then peeled off her clothes, which were clinging to her uncomfortably. The old-fashioned bath took a long time to fill, so she decided to shampoo her hair while she waited. Not for the first time she was grateful that it was the good-tempered type that needed no setting. She towelled it dry and turned off the bath taps. Her bottle of bath oil was almost empty, and she knew who was responsible for that. Dear Bernard wouldn't dream of buying any when he could scrounge hers! But as she lay in the comfort of the hot water she knew she was being ungrateful, for after the wedding-that-never-was Aunt Marian's kind invitation had been more than welcome, there was nowhere else she could have gone. As for Bernard, he was a pain in the neck, but he did have some good points at times. To be fair, she believed that in her present mood she would find something to complain about in a saint! Thank goodness she had happened to see young Brian as he fell in the river and had not been too wrapped up in her thoughts. There had been many people about, but nobody else had attempted to rescue him. Somebody would doubtless have done so eventually, but time was of the essence where a small child was concerned.

Understandably Mrs Constable had been most grateful and had issued her invitation for Sunday on the spur of the moment. But now that moment had passed. Would seeing Jennifer again bring back a memory she would prefer to forget? Maybe, though, it would be better that she remembered. In any event it would be embarrassing for Jennifer herself to be the only stranger in a group of friends and to know that the doctor was being urged to do something for an out-of-work nurse in return for a service. She could imagine how the conversation would go.

'Why on earth did you invite her here? I don't know anything about her capabilities. What does she expect me to do?'

'We must reward her, darling, and I'm sure she would appreciate your interest, and especially if you could find her something. After all, you must have some influence.'

Jennifer wondered whether she wanted to return to nursing. Wouldn't it constantly remind her of Exmouth, the curiosity, celebrations and congratulations? Besides, she had left there without giving notice in the proper way because she couldn't face her colleagues or the fact that Simon was working under the same roof. When she applied for a new job she would have a lot of explaining to do, which would be embarrassing. If Dr Constable could pull something out of his hat that might be the answer to her problem.

She heard a car arrive in the driveway and jumped out of the bath. She pulled out the plug and grabbing her towel hurried into her bedroom. It was Bernard, and if he found the bathroom occupied he would be in a foul mood for the rest of the evening. He always declared he needed a bath after teaching learner drivers all day.

His father had died a few years ago knowing full well that Marian spoiled him, and she had continued to do so and truly believed that every girl that Bernard met was 'after him', and in the course of his work he met a good few. He was quite good-looking, or could have been without that revolting mouse-coloured silky moustache which he constantly fingered as he smiled from half-closed eyes. Jennifer was pretty certain he practised that leer in front of the mirror, believing it to be sexy. He had a healthy tan and his teeth and features were not bad, but Jennifer didn't care for his eyes. They were light brown and had a surprised expression, as if he could see something strange just behind her, and she was constantly looking over her shoulder to see what it was. She really didn't like him very much—but she was obviously no good judge of character, for she had loved Simon, and see how he had turned out. Thinking of him now, he appeared indistinct and wreathed in shadows, but she didn't need to see a clear picture of him to remember him well. He was tall and lean and wore glasses. She had thought his slight stoop made him look intellectual, although in her heart she had known it was caused by being very tall. He had been generous—unlike Bernard—and had a good sense of humour. She had to admit it had a cruel, satirical vein, but she had felt flattered to share it with him. Why had he jilted her so unexpectedly? Was it something she had inadvertently done? she asked herself over and over again. The only solution she could reach was that if love can come suddenly and unbidden then maybe it could go just as easily.

For the next few days Jennifer couldn't make up her mind about Sunday. It was Saturday that decided her. It was an extremely hot day and she was serving ice-cream non-stop, feeling she was surrounded by thousands of tongues; long ones, short fat ones, pink ones, grey ones, catching ice-cream as it dripped from wafers, circling and whirling around the protruding blob in cornets, licking sticky chins and fingers. She watched them in disgust, certain now that this job was not for her, and she prayed that Dr Constable would be able to help her.

Telling her aunt and Bernard that she wouldn't be home for Sunday lunch brought disapproving stares from them both.

'But you don't know these people, and I feel responsible for you,' her aunt said with an anxious frown.

'I'm a big girl now and quite used to dealing with obstreperous patients in Casualty on a Saturday night, so I'm sure I'll be all right at a doctor's luncheon party. But if you're really worried, this is the address, and you can send out a posse of police to protect me,' Jennifer smiled, and threw the card on the table.

Bernard picked it up and after slowly reading it smoothed his moustache and said with his look of surprise.

'If they harm my girl they'll have me to reckon with, I kid you not!'

His mother gave a reproachful giggle. 'Oh, Bernard, you mustn't lead Jennifer to think she's your girl!'

Jennifer ran upstairs noisily, gritting her teeth as she went. Venting her irritation on her honey-coloured hair, she brushed it vigorously as if it had offended her. In return it formed itself into a deep wave before reaching almost to her shoulders. She wasn't sure what to wear, but settled on a cream two-piece which showed up her sun tan and dark colouring. She glanced at her reflection, and was surprised to see how healthy she looked when she felt so frail inside. Again she wondered why Simon had treated her so badly. Had she developed some new trait that had irritated him? But she couldn't believe anything very drastic had happened since he had asked her to marry him. That was eighteen months ago, and she had said she wanted to wait until she had completed her SRN exams. So had *he* changed during that time when she was busy study-ing? She knew he had become friendly with Dr

Mailer, who was an older man, but they had a common interest in sailing and Simon had spent several weekends at his Bigbury-on-Sea home. With a sudden jolt of awareness, as if a curtain had been whisked aside, she recalled that Dr Mailer had a daughter; Jennifer had sometimes seen her when she called at the hospital. She had been a pretty little schoolgirl, but schoolgirls have a habit of growing up. She was called Sheila, and one night when Simon was kissing her he'd called *her* Sheila. She tensed. At the time she had laughed and not been in the least suspicious, and because of that he might have believed she didn't care. Could Sheila Mailer be the reason for his behaviour? Not that it mattered now, but it did give her the satisfaction of a possible solution.

With a spurt of anger she took off the gold chain that Simon had given her and replaced it with blue beads and earrings. She didn't want to be reminded of him.

The Willows was within walking distance, but she walked slowly and reluctantly. It was an attractive white house covered with a green creeper and set in a well-kept garden. Several cars were parked in the drive, so presumably the friends had already arrived.

Mrs Constable opened the door to her knock and seemed genuinely pleased to see her.

'How very nice,' she smiled. 'I hope you're no worse for your drenching?'

'Oh no, I'm quite all right. And how is Brian? I hope he didn't suffer any shock?'

Mrs Constable laid her hand on Jennifer's arm. 'No, my dear, he had no after-effects at all.' She lowered her voice. 'Unlike me! It sounds an awful thing for a grandmother to say, but I'm quite relieved that his parents are home again and he's back with them. I'd forgotten how much effort it takes to look after a young child.' She gave a guilty laugh, then led her towards a tall grey-haired man who was talking to a middle-aged couple.

'Miss Langford—or may I call you Jennifer? My husband has been looking forward to meeting you.'

He turned to look at her and Jennifer was immediately aware of a warmth and comfort that emanated from him.

'So pleased to be able to thank you personally,' he said as he shook hands with her. 'Meet Mrs Cross and Dr Cross, very good friends of ours.'

After they had exchanged pleasantries he steered her towards another couple.

'Sarah, I'd like you to meet Miss Langford. Miss Betts is my excellent secretary. Indeed, I don't know what I would do without her.' He put an arm around her shoulders.

She was tall with fair hair which was brushed fashionably behind her ears. She was undeniably good-looking and smart in a grey silk dress with coral accessories.

'Hello.' Her mouth formed an attractive smile,

but her eyes were light grey, cool and watchful.

Dr Constable turned to her companion. 'Dr Grant. Roger and I are good friends, aren't we, old man, but we agree to differ on many things. Isn't that right?'

Both men laughed. Then Dr Constable said something to Sarah Betts which Jennifer didn't hear, because Roger Grant was looking down at her from his great height and she felt a strange tremor pass through her. Then he held out a hand so large that it completely enveloped hers, and to her disgusted amazement her body thrilled and tingled and her heart missed a beat. Hastily she pulled her hand away and inadvertently looked up into deep brown eyes that seemed both compelling and slightly amused. Sarah slipped her hand possessively through his arm and drew him away, murmuring something at which they both laughed.

Jennifer wished she hadn't come here; she was obviously the odd one out. But after some wine and a delicious meal she felt more relaxed. This was certainly a great improvement on being at home with Aunt Marian and Bernard. This Roger Grant obviously thought a great deal of himself—he was arrogant and immensely self-confident and spoke in a loud, commanding voice, whereas Dr Constable put his views forward quietly but firmly. Sarah was quite plainly torn between the two men, agreeing with each in turn, and was no doubt a very diplomatic secretary.

After lunch was over Dr Constable invited Jennifer into his study for a chat.

'Do sit down, my dear. First of all I must say again how grateful my wife and I are for your swift reaction to our grandson's accident. Thanks to you he suffered no ill effects. I want you to be sure to send me the bill for any damage that was done to your clothing. I understand you lost your shoes?'

'Yes, but they were quite old ones. I'm just thankful that I saw Brian in time.'

He picked up a gold pen from his mahogany desk and fiddled with it. 'Now my wife gave me to understand that you're a nurse but not employed as such at the moment. Would you like to tell me about that?'

It had never occurred to Jennifer that she would be asked that question, and for a moment she felt tongue-tied, but such was the kindliness of his manner and his gentle but authoritative air that she found herself telling him everything. When she had finished her story things did not seem so bad.

'I'm very sorry,' he said. 'It must have been a wretched experience. I can quite understand that you wouldn't want to go back to that hospital. Did you, however, write to the SNO?'

Jennifer bit her lip. 'Not right away, I—I couldn't. But a couple of weeks ago I wrote and said I was sorry I hadn't given proper notice of leaving and received a pleasant note in reply.'

He nodded. 'Good. Well, now I'll see what I can

do for you—but you will understand that I can make no promises, and in the meantime I do advise you to study the nursing journals to see if there's something suitable. You mustn't waste your training.'

He stood up and laid his hand on her shoulder. 'Difficult though this affair must have been it was better than entering into a marriage to which both partners were not entirely committed. You're young and attractive, and in time I hope you'll meet somebody who will make you happy.'

Jennifer thanked him and left shortly afterwards. It was when she said goodbye to Roger Grant that she felt a ridiculous flood of hurt, for he barely glanced at her, whereas when he had first met her he had stared hard enough. But that was a couple of hours ago, and men changed. Men! she thought disgustedly, I can do without the lot of them.

CHAPTER TWO

JENNIFER had been tired of so much relentless sunshine and nauseated by the amount of ice-cream that was being consumed, but she should have known better and counted her blessings, for now there was a spell of wet weather when holiday-makers and tourists kept away from the mist-enshrouded river and tubs of ice-cream remained unopened. This bleak change should have persuaded her to search the nursing journals for possible vacancies, but so far she couldn't bring herself to do so. She hadn't heard from Dr Constable, and that didn't surprise her. He had been pleasant and sympathetic on the surface, but that meant nothing. Men were deceivers ever, as Shakespeare said, and she had been foolish to go to that luncheon party, because it had raised her hopes. She was certainly down in the dumps, and the letter she received from her mother enclosing a newspaper cutting which announced the forthcoming marriage of Simon to Sheila Mailer, daughter of Dr and Mrs George Mailer of Broad Oaks, Exmouth, had something to do with it. So she had guessed right, it *had* been Sheila. So why hadn't Simon told her he had had a change of heart? Why leave it until the wedding day? With a flight of fancy Jennifer wondered if perhaps he had a pathological fear of marriage and would ditch Sheila too. Maybe he would go on and on doing it until he was in the *Guinness Book of Records*!

Then she received an uninteresting-looking beige letter which she pushed aside, believing it to be a circular. Bernard picked it up, studied it, then passed it to her.

'You can open it. Naughty to keep secrets from me, old girl!'

She snatched it from him and ran upstairs with it. It was a brief note from St Anselm's, the local hospital, inviting her for an interview the following afternoon.

With a mixture of hope and apprehension she locked up the kiosk early and set out for the hospital, which was within walking distance. Her way lay between rows of Victorian houses, some of which had been demolished and replaced by a few small shops and a couple of factories. The hospital was built of mellowed bricks, set back from the road and surrounded by trees and lawns, with seats for convalescent patients or staff or visitors who wished to sit and rest.

Jennifer paused at the entrance for a moment and looked around her before going through the automatic doors. Once inside she could have been back in the Exmouth hospital, with long straight corridors with rooms on either side and poster-covered walls. People hurried in all directions, nurses carried folders, porters wheeled trolleys or stretchers and in the distance was the hollow sound of voices and equipment being moved.

Jennifer saw on the indicator that the SNO's office was on the first floor. She walked through the crowded outpatients department, past the eye clinic and pathological laboratory, and squeezed into a lift which was taking a stretcher case to X-Ray. When she stepped out she saw that the SNO's office was right there.

To her surprise the SNO was a man. He questioned her about her experience and qualifications. He knew she had come from Exmouth, and she believed he knew why, but he didn't refer to it, and she was glad.

'Dr Constable spoke to me about you, and I'm pleased to be able to offer you a temporary post. It's for six months, so would you be interested in taking that?' he asked.

'Yes, please, I would,' said Jennifer gratefully.

'Right. I'd like you to start on Monday if that's possible?' He looked at her questioningly.

'Yes, I can manage that.' She thought for a moment. 'As it's a temporary post might I wear my Exmouth uniform?'

'Yes, certainly, that makes sense.'

As she was about to leave he said, 'I do urge you, in your own interest, to keep looking for a permanency elsewhere.'

On Monday she went down to breakfast wearing her brown and white checked uniform dress. Her cap and apron were neatly folded and in her holdall.

'Doesn't she look smart, Bernard?' said Aunt Marian as she poured out the tea.

He eyed her with his air of surprise and twirled the ends of his moustache.

'Ye-es, quite dishy.' He wagged his finger at Jennifer. 'But just you remember whose girl you are, or I shall have to take somewhat drastic action. D'you get my meaning?'

'Oh, Bernard!' Aunt Marian shook her head with a fond smile. 'You are a tease!'

Jennifer had been told to report to the Sister in charge of the children's ward. At one end of the corridor a large cardboard model of Miss Piggy carried a signboard pointing to the ward doors, but Jennifer went into the office beside them to announce her arrival.

Sister Boniface was young, looked jolly and welcomed Jennifer with a smile.

'Ah, Nurse Langford, welcome to St Anselm's,' she said, holding out a plump hand. 'We call each other by our first names here, for the sake of the children. I'm Rose and—' she consulted a paper on her desk, 'and I see you're Jennifer. The same applies to the doctors. Have you been accustomed to that?'

Jennifer shook her head. 'I think it's a very

friendly idea, but no, we used titles at Exmouth.'

Rose laughed. 'We're very unconventional here, thanks to our paediatrician. We allow the children to do more or less as they like. Medicines, of course, are given strictly on the dot, but we don't get the children to rest at any specific time. Doctor says that when they're tired they'll fall asleep and when they aren't there's no point in trying to make them.'

'I'm sure the children must be very happy here. Do the mothers stay with them overnight?'

Sister Boniface shook her head. 'Only in special circumstances.'

'It's a very popular practice nowadays, though, isn't it? At Exmouth we allowed them to stay.'

'There's something to be said for it, but our paediatrician—he's dead against it.'

That was a man, of course, and he wouldn't understand.

'I think women would have more sympathy with the mother staying,' Jennifer said stiffly.

'I doubt if they would have more sympathy than our doctor has. His opinion is that sometimes for one reason or another, such as there being other children at home, the mother is unable to stay much as she might like to. But the little patient sees other mothers staying and feels she isn't loved as much.'

'Of course, I hadn't thought of that,' Jennifer said slowly.

'So that's why we make that rule, generally

speaking, that none of them should stay. Have you worked with children before?'

'Only for a short while during training.'

Rose gave a wry smile. 'Then the best of luck, you'll either love it or hate it. On the whole they're a noisy bunch at the moment.' Her face shadowed. 'Unfortunately there are a few who are pretty sick and their outlook is poor, but our doctor says that's all the more reason for them to see some fun and laughter. If they were at home they'd mostly have the attention of sad, doting parents who were worried sick, and that's not a good atmosphere for a child, however ill.' She stood up. 'Are you ready to face them?'

'I think so, but I'd like to have known something about each child.'

'Their names are on their beds or cots along with their charts. 'You'll find out more by reading those than trying to remember anything I tell you. Debbie is on the ward with you, and Sandra or an agency nurse will be in this afternoon. And I'm usually somewhere around. Shall we go?'

The ward looked delightful, like a large toy shop, with trains and wheelbarrows and dolls' prams strewn across the floor. There were rag dolls and teddy-bears and stuffed animals perched on tables and chairs or in corners. On the walls were murals of farms and animals and TV characters. Children ran or staggered around, while younger ones stood in their cots holding on to the rails and watching them. A few lay pale-faced with drips inserted or with limbs in traction.

'Hello, children!' Rose shouted above the din.

A few discordant voices said, '"lo" Rose.'

'This is Jennifer, who's going to be here with you. Say Hello to her.'

'Lo, Jen—Jenfer,' they said shyly.

'Hello, children,' she replied. Then the office phone rang, and with a friendly wave Rose left her.

No sooner had she gone than the children who were able crowded around Jennifer, pulling at her dress, each speaking louder than the others to gain her attention.

'I got lumps in my froat,' a small girl said, opening her mouth wide for her inspection.

'I got spots,' said a boy, pulling up his T-shirt to reveal a scarlet rash which Jennifer was unable to identify.

'I got a nabscess!' A small boy was about to pull down his slacks to show her, but she gently stopped him, and said she'd see it when it needed a fresh dressing.

Jennifer expressed her interest in all the ailments, but her attention was caught by a little girl who sat in the far corner, her hands behind her back.

When the hubbub had subsided Jennifer crossed over to her.

'Hello, love, what's your name?'

'Wendy,' she whispered, her flaxen hair almost

hiding her face, so that Jennifer felt she would like to brush it aside.

'That's a pretty name. And do you know why you're here?' The child shook her head. 'I tell you what I'll do if you like. Shall I plait your hair so that it doesn't get in your eyes?'

The little girl nodded silently.

'Would you like two plaits or lots of little ones like Sheema has got?' Jennifer indicated the pretty little black-haired girl who wore her hair in numerous plaits each ending with some coloured beads.

Wendy eyed them warily. 'Just two,' she whispered.

When Jennifer had made the plaits she asked Wendy to hold the ends.

'I'll try and find something to tie them with. I haven't got any ribbon, but I'll buy some next time I go to the shops. What colour would you like?'

Wendy shook her head and made no move to hold the plaits.

Jennifer touched her arm. 'Will you hold them for me?'

Wendy dragged away and kept both hands determinedly behind her back.

'My, my, I don't believe you've got any hands,' Jennifer teased.

But to her dismay Wendy's eyes filled with tears. Jennifer put an arm around her. 'What's the matter, love? Don't you want your hair in plaits? Shall I undo them?'

Two large tears rolled down the little girl's cheeks and still she said nothing.

'My goodness! No hands, no tongue. Come on, let me see if you've got a tongue.' Jennifer tickled her cheeks until she opened her mouth and Jennifer peered inside. 'Why, yes, you have, you've got a nice little pink tongue. Now let me see if you've got any hands.'

'No, no!' Wendy cried, pulling away from her.

'All right, love, I'll find something to tie up your hair, then it will be all done.'

Jennifer went thoughtfully to the dressings room, where she cut strips of muslin and wondered all the while why Wendy hid her hands. Maybe she bit her nails and her parents or teacher had been angry with her, but it would do no good for her to become neurotic about it.

Later in the morning Jennifer took her a beaker of orange juice and a straw. She gave it to her casually, talking to another child as she did so. Wendy took the mug and from the corner of her eye Jennifer noticed that she had some warts on her hands. Could they be the trouble? Jennifer hesitated, not knowing whether it would be better to ignore them, but then she decided to speak.

'I see you've got some warts like I used to have when I was your age. My granny said they were fairies' footmarks and were supposed to be lucky,' she said brightly.

Wendy looked at Jennifer's hands. 'Where are they now?'

Jennifer laughed. 'I wanted them gone, so she rubbed pennywort on them and they soon went away. Yours will go too before long.'

Wendy's big blue eyes looked pleadingly at her. 'A pennyworth of what?'

Jennifer dropped a kiss on her flaxen head.

'Not a pennyworth, love, but pennywort. That's special leaves that she picked in a hedge.'

'Please ask her to get some for me. Please!' the child pleaded.

Jennifer thought sadly for a moment of the grandmother she had so loved and who had recently died.

'We use something different, nowadays, something much better. That was years ago, when I was your age.'

Again Wendy put her hands determinedly behind her back. 'No, no, I don't want what they do to them here—I won't let them!' she cried hysterically.

'Why not, Wendy? Don't you want them to go away?'

'Yes, I do, but they burn them out here—a boy at school told me so. He said they'd burn them out and leave holes. I don't want holes in my hands.' Wendy's eyes filled with tears.

'Don't you worry—nobody's going to do anything to them that you don't want them to do. But

I'll tell you something. That was a very stupid boy and he'd got it all wrong.'

'He wasn't, he wasn't, because Sharon Brown told me so too.' Tears rained down her cheeks.

'All right, darling, nobody's going to burn them, I promise.'

There was a lot of commotion as a nurse entered the ward wheeling a trolley decorated with cut-outs of animals. She looked as if she had stepped straight out of a musical comedy, with long pink ears fixed to her cap and a powder puff tail pinned on her uniform.

She greeted Jennifer with a smile. 'Hello, I believe you're Jennifer. I'm Nurse Bunny-get-you-better,' she laughed. 'In other words, this is the medicine trolley.'

Jennifer joined in her laughter. 'And you, I take it, are Debbie.'

'Right first time. So will you check the medicines with me, please.'

She was a bright-eyed girl with a dark fringe and rosy cheeks and was obviously fond of the children. The medicines were served in eggcups made like chickens or animals and were accepted readily by the children.

'Whose idea is this?' asked Jennifer.

'Our paediatrician's. He's a laugh and a law unto himself, and the kids adore him.'

Jennifer soothed a little girl who was sobbing quietly because her bed needed changing.

'Don't worry, love, we'll get you clean again in no time. It's not your fault at all.'

She washed and changed her and put a fresh draw-sheet on the bed. Then she put some saline and glucose in another child's drip and took her temperature.

A boy grizzled and said he was thirsty. He pushed over his tumbler of water and insisted that he wanted orange juice. In the centre of the ward two children struggled and fought over the possession of a bus. More cots needed changing and tears dried. After what seemed a long and tiring time Debbie suggested that Jennifer should go for coffee.

'It's down the corridor and on the left. You'll know where it is by the clatter of dishes and the smell of coffee, which, incidentally, is tenpence a cup. Fifteen minutes—OK?'

Fifteen minutes didn't give one long by the time you'd walked there and back, queued and gone to the cloakroom if you wanted to. At Exmouth it had been more lax, and provided that you didn't take advantage by staying too long, nobody checked your comings and goings. As it happened there wasn't a queue at the counter and Jennifer had time to look around for an unoccupied table—it was no use getting into conversation with anybody, the time was too short. The room was apparently for the use of all the employees from the doctors to the porters. That too was different from Exmouth, where they had separate rooms. She glanced at one table, then looked again. Surely, wasn't that Dr Grant? Or Roger, as Dr Constable had told her to call him? But no, this man couldn't be a doctor, he was wearing baggy pants, a bright blue shirt with a huge blue tie covered with large red spots and his dark hair was quite long. If he was really a doctor then he was letting down the profession.

He glanced up and saw her and raised a massive hand in greeting. She smiled politely and looked away.

'Come over here,' he called, or rather, bellowed. Jennifer felt all eyes were on her as she made her way across to him. It was no use pretending she hadn't heard, for there could scarcely be a person in the hospital who hadn't!

He half stood up and drew out a chair for her. 'Hello, Jennifer. So James pulled this place out of his hat for you.'

Jennifer looked at his face. It was strong and rugged with brown eyes that really studied you, she could almost feel them boring into her, and she felt that if she didn't lower her eyelids quickly he would know just what she was thinking. And what she was thinking was that despite his informal dress and loud manner he was outstandingly attractive, and she felt immensely flattered that he remembered her and had invited her to sit with him. Naturally she didn't want him to know that, so she stared hard at her light grey coffee.

'Yes, it was very kind of him,' she said.

'Have you known James long?' he asked.

'No, I—I met his wife, and she invited me to lunch. That was the first time I'd seen him.'

She knew he was staring at her, for two hot patches formed on her cheeks.

'You aren't—? No. Or are you? Did you fish young Brian out of the drink?'

Jennifer automatically glanced up, but quickly looked away again.

'Yes, but it was nothing. We were in and out again in a flash.'

He chuckled. 'Did you say flash? Or splash? Anyhow, good for you. Were you on holiday?'

The last thing Jennifer wanted was to have to explain to him how she had come to be there on the river bank at that moment, but she felt certain that if he wanted to know something he would jolly well ask and she would have to answer him. She turned over the fob watch which hung on her bodice and jumped quickly to her feet.

'Heavens, I must get back or I'll be late!'

She shivered as his massive hand covered hers. 'You've only just arrived.'

'But my quarter of an hour is almost up,' she explained.

He gave a loud chuckle. 'You don't want to take that too literally.'

'But I must—it's my first day here.'

'Oh yes. Well, you be a new broom, my dear.' He

picked up a newspaper, opened it, crossed massive legs and looked as if he was settling down for the day.

Some doctor! Jennifer thought as she left the dining room. Would he bestir himself if there was a crisis? She answered her own question. Not if he didn't feel like it.

Debbie greeted her with a smile. 'You've been quick. No queues?'

'No, it wasn't bad at all, but you did say fifteen minutes, didn't you?'

Debbie skidded across the floor, to rescue a tiny boy who was halfway over the rails of his cot. 'No, you don't,' she scolded, rubbing her cheek against his. 'You stay right where you are until I get you out myself. Right?'

She returned to Jennifer. 'Fifteen minutes is what it's supposed to be and what we say, but —well, it depends on circumstances. Anyhow, I'll go now, and I won't be too long as it's your first day.'

Now that she was left on her own Jennifer felt more alarmed than she had ever done since becoming a nurse. A little boy with a destructive urge rammed a wheelbarrow repeatedly against the wall. A small girl let out a piercing scream, and Jennifer hurried over to her to see how seriously she was hurt. It proved to be nothing more than a desire to gain attention. From everywhere came shouts and roars and screams, and the noise was deafening. Suddenly over the din a voice boomed.

'Hello, children!'

They turned with cries of delight and flung themselves against a huge figure wearing a blue shirt, baggy pants and a large spotted bow tie. His arms were so big they seemed to encompass them all as he patted heads, chucked chins, joked and called them by name.

'Roger, see my knee!'

'My froat's still got lumps.'

A small boy whose legs were in plaster held up his arms to him. Roger hoisted him up with infinite care.

'How are you doing, Robin? What number do I write on your plaster today? I think it's seven, isn't it?'

'No, no, Roger, it's eight!' The boy pointed to a figure seven that was already there.

'Well, blow me down, the days are flying past, aren't they? Let me write eight here, we don't want to forget, do we?' He took a pen from his pocket and wrote the figure eight. 'Now let me see, what number do we put tomorrow?'

A mischievous glint came into the boy's eyes. 'Ten,' he said slyly.

Roget Grant gave him a sideways look, then shook his head. 'I'm not sure about that, I'll have to work it out on my computer.'

He replaced the boy in his cot, then taking the chart from the end panel read it through carefully before putting it back.

'A few more days and we'll have that plaster off and take some pictures to see how those legs of yours are doing. That reminds me.' He felt in one large pocket and then in another, then took out a drawing. 'How do you like that?'

The boy laughed aloud. 'It's me, it's me, but I haven't got a big red chest.'

Roger raised his eyebrows. 'All robins have,' he said.

Jennifer felt at a loss. Hadn't he heard of protocol? Didn't he know he should consult the nurse on duty? And where was Sister Boniface?

As if he could read her thoughts Roger chose that moment to look directly at her. Taken unawares, she felt everything inside her swoop down except for her heart, which stayed right where it was and beat furiously at being abandoned.

'Anything special to report, Jennifer?'

She wanted to speak to him about Wendy's warts, but not where the children might overhear.

'I haven't been told anything in particular, but I read that Wendy is here for observation and I wondered if you'd had any results yet.'

'Ah yes—Wendy.' He strode over to the child and squatted down beside her. 'How is my sweetheart this morning?' he asked. 'Looking very smart, I must say, and grown-up too, with your hair in plaits. Who did that for you?'

Wendy dimpled. 'Jenfer. She's going to buy me

some ribbon for them.'

Roger glanced sideways at Jennifer. 'Is she indeed? And what colour will it be?'

Wendy shook her head.

'You ask for blue to match my bow, because that's my favourite colour. Now that you're such a grown-up young lady I'll tell you why you're in here, Wendy. Everybody, Jennifer, all the other children, and you and I, have two little kidneys inside us. They're very useful, they fight the germs in our bodies and keep us fit. Well, yours are lazy old things, and I'm going to ask Nurse Bunny-get-you-better to give you something to make them work harder. That'll teach them, won't it?'

Wendy nodded and smiled, but Jennifer noticed that she still kept her hands out of sight.

Roger spent time talking to each child, explaining as much as possible why they were in hospital and what was being done for them.

Debbie returned and Sister Boniface came into the ward, but it was quite plain that Roger Grant's main concern was to ensure that the children were included in whatever was said about them and their condition. It seemed odd to Jennifer that he had overlooked Wendy's preoccupation with her hands.

As he was leaving the ward Jennifer hurried after him and caught up with him just outside.

'Roger——' she began hesitantly, because it seemed strange to be so familiar.

He looked questioningly at her from his great height.

'I'd like to speak to you about one of the children, but not here, please.'

'Then where do you suggest we meet?'

'Somewhere private,' she said, and at his glance felt the colour rush into her cheeks.

'That sounds promising,' he said, his eyes smiling.

'No, please, it's important—only I don't want the children to hear.'

'Then I'll see you in my office. It's on the first floor and I should be there at three o'clock. Tell Rose I've asked to see you. OK?'

He greeted a doctor who was passing and they walked away together.

At exactly three o'clock Jennifer knocked on his door, and although she was prepared to hear his loud reply the actual sound made her jump. He glanced up briefly when she entered, said he wouldn't be a minute, and continued his large left-handed scrawl.

'Sit down, please,' he commanded, then read through what he had written and placed it in a tray.

'So now,' he said, leaning bare arms on his desk, 'what can I do for you?'

'It's Wendy's hands,' said Jennifer. 'I don't know if you've noticed them?'

'Noticed her hands? I'd have noticed if she hadn't got any. What are you talking about?'

She wished he wasn't so large, or so noisy, it made her feel claustrophobic, as if she had to move away from him, and yet there was that magnetic pull which made her want to draw closer. He looked at her intently with those dark brown eyes that saw everything but told you nothing.

'They've got warts on them,' she explained.

'Warts? That's nothing, they're not painful, are they?'

'I don't think so. They may mean nothing to you, but Wendy is very concerned about them. She hides her hands behind her back. Haven't you noticed?'

'Hides them? What on earth for?'

'Because she thinks they're ugly.'

With a great sweep of his arm Roger pushed papers aside as if they were of no consequence. 'You ladies think too much of your appearance. At her age they shouldn't concern her at all. By the time it might matter they'll have disappeared and not even be a memory.'

'But they *do* concern her!' protested Jennifer, her eyes darkly blue with intensity.

'Do they? Then we'll remove them, but it's hardly worth the bother, I should have thought.'

Jennifer bit her bottom lip and tilted her head to one side. 'She insists she won't have them treated here because some silly boy told her they burn them out and leave holes, and she believed him.'

He gave a loud guffaw. 'Poor kid! She thinks she'll have hands like a colander? That sounds horrific. However, it leaves us where we are. If she doesn't like her warts and refuses to have treatment for them there's not a lot we can do.'

Jennifer chewed the tip of her thumb thought-fully. 'Well, there is, you see. I told her that my grandmother cured mine with the juice of penny-wort. So—so couldn't we do that for her?' she ended with a rush.

'Pennywort? Pennywort? You must be joking!'

'I'm not. My grandmother believed that in nature there was a cure for everything. And so do I. I mean, that's why dock leaves are nearly always found growing near stinging nettles, because the juice of them takes away the sting.'

'My dear girl, there are sprays and lotions and ointments for stings which you can buy at any pharmacist's. People can't go hunting for weeds in the faint hope of finding something that would do the job.' Roger spoke as if that was the end of the matter.

'I'm not saying everything can be cured that way, but I do believe quite a number of things can. My grandmother said they grew thyme beside the cow-sheds to keep flies away, and that was better than the sprays you can buy that are not only expensive but can pollute the air.'

Roger leaned his chin on his fist and waited for her to continue as she warmed to the subject. 'Then there's digitalis from foxgloves which, as you know, is used for heart conditions.'

He nodded. 'Yes, it can be useful in cases of auricular fibrillation.'

'And there's camomile tea, used for colic and some shampoos.'

He laughed. 'I wonder what the common denominator is between muscular spasms and hair?'

Jennifer gave him a sharp glance. 'This isn't a laughing matter. Then there are poppyseeds.'

'What about them?'

She looked at him dubiously, wondering if he was teasing her.

'She said if you boiled them for a quarter of an hour they made a marvellous fomentation for relieving pain.'

Roger leaned closer. 'Tell me more.'

'And saffron, which comes from crocus, will bring out the rash in measles, and—and there are lots of others too.'

'I'll tell you something else,' he said. 'You can sprinkle poppyseeds on bread and if you live in Cornwall you can put saffron in cakes. And if you stand under a sprig of mistletoe you can kiss the lady of your choice without having your face slapped,' he ended with a laugh.

She turned aside in disappointment. 'Oh, you're impossible!'

He leaned closer. 'Did your granny also use eye of newt and toe of frog?' He was now so close that she could see that the tip of each eyelash, and in the iris of his eyes was a touch of gold. She realised she was staring, fascinated, and forced herself to turn aside.

'I'm being serious. Couldn't we please try penny-wort on Wendy?'

He shrugged massive shoulders. 'You can try what you like if it pleases you.'

A light shone in her eyes and brought colour to her cheeks. 'Oh, good. Thank you very much. Do—do you know where I can find some?'

'Do *I* know?' he roared. 'I don't know anything about the stuff. That, my dear, is your province.'

'Well, you see, I don't know this part of the country. In Devonshire pennywort grows in stone hedges. Are there any like that around here?'

Roger stared at her thoughtfully for a moment, his eyes travelling over her from her sleek fair hair to her widely-spaced blue eyes, over her heart-shaped face, then to her slim but shapely body and back again to her eyes.

Jennifer felt as if he had actually touched every part of her, and a delicious thrill ran through her.

He smiled. 'As it apparently means so much to you and Wendy, we'll try and find some. When are you off duty?'

'Off duty? On—on Thursday,' she said.

'Right. I'll meet you at two-thirty in the car park, and we'll search for this magic herb.'

He gave loud laugh as she closed the door, and she stood and covered her face with her hands. What could you do with a man like that?

CHAPTER THREE

JENNIFER sat in a Windsor café drinking coffee and watching the tourists who lounged on the grassy slope outside the fairy-tale castle, one of nine which William the Conqueror had erected. One day she really must go on a guided tour of the Castle, and she wished it were possible to take the children in her ward to see Queen Mary's Doll's House, which was made in 1923. How they would love it, because it was said that almost all the tiny gadgets worked, the vacuum cleaner, sewing machine and gramophone. Even the lifts worked, and the two pianos. The wine in the miniature bottles in the wine cellar would have improved with age—not that anyone would ever sample it.

She had mixed feelings about this afternoon, when she and Roger Grant were going to look for some pennywort, which she hoped they would find. She felt apprehensive because she knew so little about him and wondered what they could talk about. But she also felt an inner excitement at the prospect of getting to know him better, for there was something about him which, whether you liked him or not, was impossible to ignore. He had such authority and obviously didn't care a fig for other people's opinion. He was large and casual, and said and did what he wanted. He was like a bulldozer, but she felt sure that whatever he did would be good. She gave a wry smile. Here she was making a thumbnail sketch of him, when she scarcely knew him!

Picking up her handbag, she prepared to leave the café. She had come here to Windsor to buy a pair of sandals to replace those that had been lost in the river. She stood in the doorway looking to right and to left, wondering where she would find a shoe shop, when with a start of surprise she saw Roger and Sarah Betts walking along on the opposite pavement. They made a striking-looking couple, both so tall and well-built. He was wearing a green and white checked shirt with an open neck and short sleeves; she, a beautifully-cut lilac two-piece, which suited her blonde colouring to perfection. She wore accessories of beads, handbag and shoes in a contrasting shade of mauve, and people passing them glanced, then looked again. Jennifer watched until they were lost in the crowd. For no apparent reason she felt flat. Her former excited anticipation vanished, and she wished she had never mentioned pennywort to Roger.

This afternoon was going to be a boring chore for him, something beyond the call of duty, taking out a relatively unknown nurse to search for something for one of his many patients, something in which he had little faith. With a sudden pang she wondered whether Sarah Betts would accompany them.

When she found a shoe shop she looked longingly at the sandals in pretty pastel shades. To choose a pair and buy a handbag and beads to match need not be all that expensive. But when she tried to decide on a colour she realised they would only look good with one particular outfit, and she needed sandals that would go with anything, so she chose a pair of beige and white strapped ones.

Bernard was at home when she arrived for lunch. She changed into a checked blouse over beige slacks and realised she was copying Roger, but she couldn't hope to emulate Sarah.

'So it's your day off. I can't promise, but I might get home early, then we can have a bit of a chinwag,' said Bernard, as if bestowing a favour.

'Sorry, I'm going out this afternoon with one of our doctors,' Jennifer replied, with a glimmer of pleasure.

He gave her his surprised half-smile. 'I've got it! Say no more. One of the nurses' perks, eh?' He fondled his moustache.

'That's right,' she agreed, tensing her muscles, and saw an unpleasant glint in his eyes.

But if this was one of the nurses' perks you could keep it, Jennifer thought later as she waited for Roger in the car park. The minutes ticked by and still there was no sign of him. Was this going to be the story of her life? Was she once more going to be brushed aside as if she was of no consequence? She closed her eyes and could see again the church, and the waiting bridesmaids, smell the scent of the flowers in her bouquet and feel again the sickness in her stomach. There must be something about her, to make men treat her like this. She looked at her watch again. He was ten minutes late. Should she leave? She decided to give him five more minutes. They seemed like hours, and her feet were leaden as she walked away. She paused at the exit, her eyes blurred.

The loud blast of a horn made her turn around. A large figure stood beside a car and bellowed,

'Hi, Jennifer, over here!'

She hesitated. She didn't want to walk meekly over to him, but she knew he could easily reach her in half a dozen strides, so she joined him reluctantly.

'Of course, you didn't know which car was mine—I'd forgotten that. Hop in.'

Jennifer felt pretty certain he hadn't been in the car park all the time, but what was the use of saying anything?

He seemed to be overlapping his seat and she drew away. 'I'd like to have the window open, please,' she said.

'Certainly.' He leaned across her and his hairy arm brushed hers as he wound down the window. 'Is that better? Right. Now we've got to find some pennywort, haven't we?'

'That was the idea,' she said coolly.

With his hands on the wheel Roger looked at her questioningly. 'So what the heck does it look like?'

'Oh, don't you know? The leaves are dark and round, slightly concave and measure about three centimetres across. Or less, if they're little ones.'

He chuckled. 'That figures. And more if they're bigger, I suppose.'

She frowned. 'They're not likely to be bigger. They're thick and juicy and grow in small clumps in stone walls back home.'

'So that's what we're hoping to find. But the only West Country thing around here is that burr in your voice.'

Jennifer looked surprised. 'I don't speak West Country, do I?'

'Of course you do. And I bet that granny of yours, besides making her witch's brew, made apple dumplings and you ate them with cream until it came out of your ears. Right?'

'Wrong.' She looked down at her waistline. 'I'm not too fat, am I?'

Roger smiled. 'You're wholesome, just right. I'm not fond of the anorexic look. So tell me about your granny.'

'Granny? She lived with us and practically brought me up, because Mother was a teacher. But none of your suet dumplings and things like that, she was practically a vegetarian—and between you and me, I grew to hate the sight of salads.'

'I'm not too fond of them either,' Roger confessed. 'But tell me about her remedies. Who knows, I might learn something to my advantage.'

Jennifer laughed. 'I doubt it. I feel sure you wouldn't take anything you didn't like, but I jolly well had to. In the winter she cut up swedes and onions and put them in a basin layered with soft brown sugar, them left it until the juice ran out, and I had to have a spoonful night and morning to ward off colds.'

'And did it work?'

'I think it must have done, because I don't remember having many coughs or colds. But I bet I smelled pretty horrible. Just imagine—swedes and onions!'

'Mm, I wonder.' Roger was silent for a few minutes as if weighing up the pros and cons of the matter. Then he said, 'What else did she make?'

'Oh heavens, let me think now,' Jennifer laughed. 'I remember she didn't believe in thermometers, but she'd look at you and know immediately if you had a temperature and if you had she'd cut up a stick of rhubarb, if it was the right time of year, I suppose, pour boiling water on it and some sugar, cover it and leave it to stand for an hour or two. Then she'd strain it, make you drink the water, and then pronounce you cured.'

'And were you?'

Jennifer shrugged. 'I'm still here.'

'True.' He glanced down at her, his brown eyes

travelling slowly over her. 'And looking very well in the bargain.'

He drove on into the pleasant countryside, but a passing glance at the hedges assured Jennifer that pennywort was unlikely to be growing in them.

'I do hope we find some,' she said.

'Did it really cure your warts?'

'Well, actually I only had one, but it was under my thumbnail and was in a difficult place to treat, and very painful, so Granny picked these leaves and told me to rub them on as often as possible.'

'You must have been what's known as a biddable child,' observed Roger.

'Oh yes, I always did what I was told. To good purpose in this case, because the wart disappeared in a couple of weeks.'

'So your granny really was a witch!'

'If you say so. But she was a very nice witch and could solve your problems as well as your ills as a rule.'

Jennifer closed her eyes. If her grandmother had been alive at the time of her 'wedding' what would her advice have been? Would she have told her beforehand not to go through with it? That Simon was not the right man for her? And if she had done so would Jennifer have believed her? Might not this have been the one occasion when she rejected her advice? In all probability, for so many friends had said that she and Simon made a perfect pair, that they were just right for each other. She had thought so too, but apparently Simon hadn't.

'Did you get the ribbon for Wendy's hair?' Roger's voice shook her into the present.

'Oh yes, and a difficult job that proved to be, thanks to you.'

'To me? I had nothing to do with it,' he protested.

'She insisted she wanted a ribbon just like your bow tie, she called it your bow,' Jennifer laughed.

'And did you manage to match it?'

'Sort of. Yours has outsize spots, but hers has tiny red dots on a blue background and I thought I was very lucky to get it.'

He glanced at her with a teasing grin. 'So I'll wear a different one just to confuse you both,' he threatened.

'Don't you be so mean,' she protested indignantly. 'Incidentally, why do you wear a bow tie like that? A small one I can understand, but yours are colossal!'

'I ask you, would a small bow tie look right on me? I don't wear an ordinary tie because I don't much fancy getting the ends mixed up in gruel or mashed banana or grabbed by sticky hands. Satisfied?'

He braked so suddenly that Jennifer was flung forward, saved by her seat belt.

'Do you always drive like that?' she demanded.

'I wasn't driving, I was stopping,' he said blandly.

'I thought this hedge looked promising. Hop out and we'll have a look.'

They wandered slowly along the lane, he searching the top of the hedge, she the bottom. After a while Jennifer shook her head.

'They don't really grow in this sort of hedge, more in a stone wall like we get in the West Country—you know, a drystone wall without any cement in the crevices. I don't think you've got any up here. But never mind, I'll ask my mother to send me some if you wouldn't mind my using it on Wendy.'

'Not at all, you go right ahead. I'm in favour of anything that will make the kids happy. You ask why I wear such large bow ties—well, it's because they like them and sometimes laugh at them. That sort of laughter is friendly, and I want to be their friend. That's why I never wear a white jacket, because that sets you apart as a doctor figure. I just want to be Roger, their friend, who they know will do all he can to help them.'

Jennifer felt a warm flood of admiration. 'And you've succeeded. It's obvious they all adore you.'

He shook his head and frowned in the strong sunlight. 'I don't want to be adored. To adore someone sets that person on a pedestal, and we come back to the fact that I want to be one of them, their best friend, if you like.'

As they returned to the car Jennifer said thoughtfully, 'You know, I find it awfully hard to understand why someone as caring of the children as you are could have failed to notice Wendy's warts.'

Roger shrugged impatiently. 'They're so utterly trivial.'

'But not to her,' Jennifer protested.

'No, I see that now. But that poor child is suffering from kidney failure, so what the hell do a few warts matter?'

She stood still, her eyes wide with dismay. 'Oh, how dreadful! I didn't know—I had no idea.'

His voice was gentler. 'Of course you didn't. I've only just been given the results of her tests.'

'Poor little girl. How—how did it come about?'

'From sheer bad luck. She contracted a virus that infected her kidneys. Her mother said she was normally a bright child and well developed for her age. To see her now, she's more like a five- or six-year-old.'

'She certainly is—and come to think of it, I've treated her that way. So what happens now?'

'She'll be on dialysis twice a week and we'll see how she gets on.'

'She's such a dear, gentle little girl,' sighed Jennifer. 'I do hope she'll be all right.'

Roger nodded. 'Get that pennywort sent up as soon as you can.'

'Pennywort?' She looked bewildered. 'But what good will that do?'

'I want her to be happy,' he said softly.

The car was cruelly hot to the touch. Roger left

the doors open and rolled down the windows to allow it to cool down a little.

'I'll never forget the time a distraught mother came running into Casualty with a baby in her arms. She'd left it in her car while she went to the shops. It took longer than she'd anticipated, but she wasn't too worried because she'd left the car locked. When she got back the car was like an oven and her baby was dead.'

'Oh, Roger, are you trying to cheer me up or something? That was a terrible story!'

'It was a terrible accident. The mother had to be admitted suffering from shock. She couldn't believe the baby had died from heat. And yet, you know,' he said thoughtfully, 'you so often read in the papers that dogs have been overcome by heat when left in cars. It's surprising she didn't think.'

Jennifer sighed. 'I know. But time goes so quickly when you're shopping that you don't realise how time is passing. And often there's a bit of a breeze, which makes it seem cooler than it would be in the car. It's so easy to judge with hindsight.'

He smiled. 'That's true. Now we'll drive down to the river and have a cup of tea to freshen us up. Unless of course you can suggest one of Granny's potions which might do us more good?'

She wrinkled her nose at him. 'Tea will do fine.'

By not honeymooning in Spain she had not missed out weatherwise. She wondered if Simon and Sheila were there at this moment. She wondered too if he had given Sheila the sapphire and diamond ring which she had posted back to him. Quite desperately she hoped not, or she would feel that a small part of herself was at their lovemaking, making her into a Peeping Tom. Dr Mailer was a wealthy man and Sheila was his only child, so apparently Simon would have no money worries now or in the future. He might even be able to set up his own dental practice. Was that why he had switched his affections? It would have eased her hurt pride to have believed so, but in all fairness she knew Simon was not a money-lover. Or was he? She had been mistaken over so much, maybe she was wrong in this too.

She realised that she was being no company for Roger and so seemed to be taking his kindness for granted.

'You've been very kind in giving up your time this afternoon and I'm sure you have plenty to do. So would you prefer to drop me off home? It's quite near here,' she said.

'Spoken like a polite little lady,' he boomed. 'But I also have time off, and I'm quite enjoying myself.'

Jennifer could see the shimmering silver ribbon of water in the distance and her spirits rose. Roger found a parking spot near a stall where they sold tea.

'It would be nice to sit out on the bank if you don't mind having a cup in your hand?'

'No, that's great.'

'Do you want anything to eat?'

Jennifer shook her head. 'No, a cup of tea will do fine.'

'Well, park yourself somewhere and I'll get it.'

She found a place where they could lie back and relax. Roger returned with the tea and a packet of biscuits. He spilt some tea on her as he passed her the cup, but seemed oblivious of the fact. She wondered how Sarah Betts would have reacted if it had happened to her and splashed her lovely lilac dress, but of course that would never come to pass, for they would take tea in a hotel or restaurant where she would be in her right setting.

As for herself, she preferred it here; the tea was good, and she lay back and closed her eyes, seeing the gold of the sun through her lids and feeling the sting of it on her arms and face.

She was miles away in her thoughts when she felt something wet dribbling on her eyelids.

'Ouch! What's that?' She tried to open her eyes, only to find that a huge hand was covering them.

'That,' Roger whispered in her ear, 'was the juice of love-in-idleness, and when you open your eyes you'll fall in love with the first living creature you see.' He removed his hand and she was looking into his velvety brown eyes. His face was so close it was almost touching hers.

She laughed delightedly. 'Forsooth, should I therefore fall in love with an ass?'

He gave her a friendly shove with his elbow that knocked her sideways.

'How was I to know you'd know *A Midsummer Night's Dream?* And who are you calling an ass?' He placed a large forefinger on her small pert nose.

'And why are you calling cold tea love-in-idleness?' Jennifer pushed his hand away.

Roger rolled over towards her. 'Do you want me to tell you?' he asked gently, and she felt an unwanted thrill of desire run through her veins.

The feeling abruptly died away, to be immediately replaced by another. This time it was of anger and disgust at both herself and him. This morning he'd been out with Sarah, his girl-friend, and this afternoon he was flirting with Jennifer and she with him, there was no doubt about that. He probably thought she would be flattered by his attentions —he a doctor and she just a nurse. Well, he was wrong. She knew how it felt to be the cheated girl and she wasn't going to be a party to deceiving Sarah. Men! They were all alike. She had no time for them, they were insincere and would happily play fast and loose with any girl who was stupid enough to be willing.

She turned her head aside and sat up. 'Thank you for taking me out and for the tea. Now I really must be getting back,' she said coolly and firmly.

'Must you?' Roger leaned back lazily on folded arms.

'Yes. I'm meeting my boy-friend.'

His eyes narrowed against the sunlight as he looked up at her.

'Congratulations, that was quick work. You haven't been in this area five minutes!'

In her guilt she was super-sensitive and believed he was doubting her.

'I'm a quick worker,' she said flippantly, and started to walk towards the car.

He caught up with her in a couple of strides. 'That's just my bad luck,' he said regretfully.

Jennifer tossed her hair back and glared resentfully ahead. Men!

CHAPTER FOUR

SOME OF the children had been discharged today, so Jennifer and Debbie were stripping and making up the beds.

'Roll on Saturday,' said Debbie.

'Saturday? Why? Are you off for the weekend?'

'No, it's the party.'

Jennifer unfolded a clean draw-sheet. 'What party's that?'

'You know—Sister Firth's.'

'Sister Firth? I've never even heard of her. You forget I'm a new girl and unless someone is working on this ward, as far as I'm concerned, they don't even exist. So what's she having a party for? Is she getting married or something, poor soul?'

Debbie shot her a look. 'She's already married. Her husband is going to Zimbabwe as a teacher and she's going with him as a nurse.'

Jennifer shook a plump pillow into a case. 'I wouldn't say that would appeal to me much. Does it you?'

'If I had a husband going with me I wouldn't mind.'

'Mm, that would make a difference, I suppose. Where's the party being held?'

'Usual place—Outpatients. I've got a new dress I'm dying to wear, so wild horses wouldn't keep me away.'

They moved on to the next bed in silence. Jennifer's thoughts were on the party when she and Simon had been the toast of the evening. It was when he had given her that lovely square-cut sapphire and diamond ring, and she had been so proud, so aware of it, that her left hand had felt as if it were outsize and didn't really belong to her.

'You'll be coming, won't you?' asked Debbie as they turned the mattress and picked up the used sheets and put them in the bin.

Jennifer forced her thoughts back to the present. 'I shouldn't think so, I wouldn't know anyone there.'

'You'd know me. Come with me if you like,' Debbie suggested generously. 'It's the best way to get to know the others. The only way, really, unless you're working with them.'

Jennifer was well aware that that made sense; she also knew that she couldn't expect Debbie to stay glued to her side all evening, for she was a friendly and popular girl. Roger would probably be there and see that she was on her own, and she didn't want him to think she was in need of friends. For already it seemed to her that he was beginning to get too friendly, and she wasn't going to fall into that trap, not even if there hadn't been Sarah to consider.

'Roger!'

The children's cries of welcome were deafening. As usual they crowded around him, and he spoke to them all, teasing them, ruffling their hair and making them laugh.

Jennifer was wheeling away the bin when a shiver ran down her spine as she felt Roger's large firm arm across her shoulders. She swung around and saw, with mixed feelings, that his other arm was on Debbie, who was smiling completely unselfconsciously.

'And how are my two favourite nurses?' he asked.

'Blooming,' Debbie replied. 'I'm trying to persuade Jennifer to come to Firth's party on Saturday. Lend your weight to my persuasions or she'll be stuck at home thinking nobody loves her.'

He looked down at Jennifer, his dark brown eyes gently caressing.

'We can't have that, can we, Debbie?'

But Debbie had gone to attend to one of the babies. Seeing that they were alone, he said,

'Do come.' And Jennifer felt the increased pressure of his hand.

She said too brightly, 'I'll have to see if my boy-friend is free.'

Roger looked at her for what seemed a long time but could only have been a couple of seconds. She felt the blood rushing to her cheeks and cursed herself for blushing. It always made her feel so

embarrassed. It was no use telling herself that it was
her body pumping out adrenalin which made some
blood vessels relax and others contract, because
that piece of knowledge learned at early lectures
didn't help at all.

Fighting to control her breath so that she could
speak naturally, she said in a garbled way,

'I rubbed some pennywort on Wendy's warts
today—it came first post. The trouble is, Wendy
expected them to disappear immediately. If they
don't ever get cured by it, I don't know what I'll
do.' She gave a rueful smile.

'Not doubting Granny's remedies, surely?' He
cocked an eyebrow.

'No cure is infallible,' she replied.

'That's the trouble, isn't it?' He strolled across to
the little pale-faced girl, who held both her hands
out to him.

'Jenfer rubbed leaves on them and soon they'll
be all gone,' she told him confidently.

Roger took her hands in his. 'Is that so? Well, I'll
let you into a secret. I've become very fond of those
little warts, so I hope they won't go away too soon.'
He lifted one of her plaits. 'My, my, what a smart
young lady—and what a pretty ribbon!'

Wendy grabbed his bow tie with both hands.
'Like yours,' she said.

He squinted down at his own. 'Why, so it is.
You've copied me.'

One moment he was there and the next he had

gone without a word of farewell, and the ward seemed empty, to Jennifer, but she knew she was being extremely foolish.

As the day wore on her mind kept returning to the party. It would be a nice change from just sitting at home watching the television when, as it was Saturday, the programmes were seldom to her liking. She had a lovely shade of cinnamon silk dress with tiny pleats which she had bought for her trousseau, and if she kept away from parties too long it would become out of date. And yet when she had foolishly mentioned her boy-friend Roger had looked so deeply into her eyes that she could almost believe he knew he was non-existent. She shrugged impatiently. How ridiculous she was! How could he possibly know, had she so little self-confidence left that she considered no one would think her sufficiently attractive to have a boy-friend? At last she came to a reluctant decision.

'Bernard,' she said that evening, at supper, 'how do you fancy coming to a party on Saturday night?'

'A party?' He stroked his moustache fondly.

'Yes, you know—cats and drinks, etcetera,' Jennifer said impatiently.

'Dear girl, I know what a party is, I've probably been to more than you've had hot dinners. But where is this merrymaking going to be held? And why?'

'At the hospital, for a Sister who's leaving, but

that needn't concern you or me. Do you want to come?'

'I should go, Bernard, I expect you'd enjoy it. There'll probably be more girls than men, and they'd be pleased to have you there.' His mother eyed him fondly.

He gave a smirk, and Jennifer steeled herself to look at the way his mouth turned down at the corners whenever he did that. He half-closed his eyes in his practised mannerism. 'I'll give it my consideration. I suppose it would be naughty of me to disappoint the little ladies.'

Jennifers' stomach rebelled and she wished she hadn't asked him. She knew he would come, and he did. Reluctantly she had to admit that he looked quite attractive. He was tall and well built, thanks to the exercise bicycle and chest expanders in his room. There was a wave in his neat, glossy hair and he was tanned—goodness knew why, as he spent his days in cars. Jennifer pushed aside the desire to wet her handkerchief and see if anything rubbed off. He wore an immaculate grey suit, white shirt and maroon tie, and she felt horribly guilty, for he had made an effort to look his best so as not to let her down and all she could do was criticise him in her mind. She determined to make up for it and try to be nice to him.

She looked at the dress which she had bought to wear on her honeymoon and suddenly knew she couldn't wear it tonight. Instead she took a far from new scarlet dress from her wardrobe, used a matching lipstick and brushed her hair until it shone. She looked at herself defiantly in the mirror and told her reflection that she was jolly well going to act as if she felt as bright as she looked.

'You do look nice, Bernard—doesn't he, Jennifer?' Aunt Marian said, eyeing him admiringly.

'He certainly does—I'll have to watch out, won't I?' Jennifer joked.

Aunt Marian dragged her eyes away from her son. 'You look nice too, that colour suits you.'

As Jennifer had thought, the party was peopled with strangers, and for once she was grateful for Bernard's presence. Dance music played in the background, but dancing on the well-trodden floor of Outpatients was not going to be all that good. Bernard fetched some red wine which Jennifer noticed clashed horribly with her dress, but drinking it was something to do. Bernard's eyes roamed the room until they came to rest, and brightened.

'There's a good-looker,' he said. 'Just the type I could go for in a big way.'

Jennifer followed his gaze, and there was Sarah Betts looking stunning in a cream crêpe dress which accentuated her splendid figure, and with kingfisher blue shoes, bracelets and beads. And beside her was Roger, looking as Jennifer had never seen him before in a well-cut brown suit, cream shirt and a cinnamon tie with a thin stripe in kingfisher blue.

As she looked at him her heart seemed to swell, then contract as she saw him and Sarah as a couple. They looked so right together. That tie must have been chosen by Sarah for just such an occasion as this, and Jennifer guessed it was because of her persuasion that he was dressed as he was. How clever that she had succeeded in doing that!

'Hello, so you decided to come.' Debbie, looking bright and cheerful in a becoming floral dress, came up beside them.

'Debbie, how nice you look. Yes, I persuaded Bernard to come. Say hello to each other, my children.'

Debbie looked with interest at Bernard, but after the briefest of glances at her he continued to stare at Sarah.

'My, have you seen our Roger?' laughed Debbie. 'I hardly recognised him!'

'They both look super,' Jennifer said slowly.

'They certainly do. Mind you, Sarah always looks ace. It must cost her a bomb to dress like that, but she's probably loaded. I adore those accessories, they make all the difference, don't they?'

Bernard glanced at Debbie then. 'Are you talking about that girl over there?'

'Yes, that's Sarah Betts with our beloved Dr Grant. He's in charge of our ward.'

Bernard stroked his moustache daintily with his forefinger. 'Roger Grant? I've heard of him.'

'Most people have around these parts. He's very

popular, especially with the children.'

Some people were dancing now and Debbie stood swaying and snapping her fingers in time to the music.

'Why don't you two join in?' suggested Jennifer.

Bernard gave her his look of surprise. 'Are you sure you wouldn't mind?'

'Of course not,' she said, and saw Debbie's eyes sparkle.

Jennifer fetched another drink and a prawn vol-au-vent and managed to find a vacant chair.

'Hello, Jennifer. Enjoying yourself?'

She looked up into the dark brown eyes which always made her feel weak.

'Not particularly, I'm not very fond of parties,' she confessed.

'So your boy-friend couldn't come?' His low voice was too smooth and his expression was challenging.

'Oh yes, I wouldn't have come without him. He's dancing with Debbie at the moment.' She'd never imagined she would be glad to say Bernard was her boy-friend!

Roger stared around the room. 'Oh, over there?' He sounded impressed.

But what Jennifer noticed was that there was a button missing from his cuff, and she felt a strange emotion. Some men would have cursed on seeing the loss and worn another shirt; others would have got Sarah to sew it on. But Roger? She doubted whether he even noticed it wasn't there. He certainly looked handsome dressed like this, but somehow he wasn't Roger. He was staring hard at her, and she glanced down at her dress to see if anything was wrong, then looked at him questioningly.

'I was just wondering how I could make use of you dressed like that,' he explained.

'Make use of me? Whatever do you mean?'

He laid his hand on her shoulder. 'Could you be Fairy Red Pencil in the ward for something or other?'

'Oh, you are rude! The other day you spoke as if I was too fat. Wholesome, was what you said. And today you imply that I'm pencil-thin,' she protested, smiling.

'Nothing of the kind—you look lovely,' he assured her.

She swallowed a huge lump in her throat. 'Where's Sarah? I saw her just now looking beautiful as usual.'

'Sarah?' Roger glanced over his shoulder. 'She's over there talking to Ian Mather, one of our consultants. He's probably finding out all he can about Dr Constable's Harley Street practice. I've got a feeling he's got a hankering in that direction.'

'Which direction? Sarah's or Harley Street?' Jennifer had spoken without thinking, and now she wished she hadn't.

Roger looked as if he wished she hadn't, too. 'Both, I suspect,' he said.

'Then shouldn't you be over there with her?' The wine had loosened her tongue.

'Why? I wanted to speak to you, as you were on your own.'

'How thoughtful of you. But here come Debbie and Bernard. Hello, you two. It's hard going on that floor, isn't it?'

'Not if your leg muscles are in good trim, old girl. So this is the Dr Grant Debbie's been enthusing about, hm?'

Jennifer introduced them to each other reluctantly. Then Bernard said to Roger,

'Where's your young lady? I saw her just now. You're taking a bit of a risk, aren't you, old boy? Letting a gorgeous creature like that out of your sight?'

Roger eyed him steadily. 'One has to take risks, don't you agree? I was just going to ask Jennifer to dance. So if you don't mind——?'

'No, no, be my guest,' said Bernard with that dreadful smirk.

'So that's your boy-friend,' Roger remarked after a few minutes.

Jennifer would have given a lot to be able to deny it, but she couldn't. 'Sarah's stopped talking to Dr Mather now, hadn't you better join her?' she asked, eyeing her admiringly as she sat cross-legged, the slit in her skirt revealing their shapeliness.

He looked down at Jennifer as if he was going to reply. Then the music changed. Swinging out an arm, he drew her so close that she felt embarrassed, aware that Sarah might be watching.

'You mustn't do that,' she said hastily, trying to pull away.

'You're a funny little thing, aren't you?' With a few long strides he danced her back to where she had been sitting. With a mock bow he thanked her, nodded to Debbie and Bernard, then walked away. Jennifer watched him as he rejoined Sarah.

To her surprise Roger danced with her again as the evening was drawing to a close. This time it was a waltz, and although it was heaven being held in his arms it was also hell, for she knew she shouldn't be there. He was probably using her to make Sarah jealous. That was what men were like—he had even admitted as much earlier on. 'I wonder how I could make use of you', he'd said. Oh, he had pretended to be joking, but that was obviously the way his mind worked.

'How did you enjoy the party?' Jennifer asked Bernard as they were walking home. It was such a lovely night and the hospital so close that he hadn't used the car.

He didn't speak for a moment. Then, holding her arm too tightly, he said,

'I don't know how you can ask that. In fact I think I should spank you.'

She shrivelled inside. *'What?'*

'I said you deserved to be spanked, the way you carried on with Roger Grant.'

'I don't know what you're talking about,' she gasped in outrage. 'He danced with me twice because we work together. He had Sarah Betts with him, he certainly didn't want me.'

'That's not to say that you didn't want him! You're a teasing puss, aren't you?' Bernard gave her a smart slap on her bottom. 'I know you only did it to vex me. But you'd better beware— Dr Roger Grant has quite a reputation in the neighbourhood.'

'Roger? A reputation? Rubbish, you don't know anything about him. I only introduced you to him tonight.'

'I told you earlier on that the name was familiar. When it comes to gossip in Henley yours truly has his ear to the ground. Don't forget I spend most days with talkative young ladies who like to confide in me.'

'How horrible! So what gossip have you heard about Roger?' Jennifer asked reluctantly.

He squeezed her arm so tightly that she winced. 'Now we're getting to the crux of it, aren't we? It seems he makes up to girls, then drops them as soon as he's had his fun. So you'd better watch out! We wouldn't want you to be tarnished goods, would we?'

She wanted to hit out at him, scream that he was lying. But the sadly disillusioned part of her mind decided reluctantly that he was probably speaking the truth.

CHAPTER FIVE

'IT'S TIME for dialysis again, Wendy my love.'

Jennifer's heart ached as she saw how weak and listless Wendy had become. She checked her weight and made a note of it, as it was essential that the blood which went into the machine from her artery and was returned to her vein after the poisonous substances had been diffused and purified by the fluid in the machine was more or less the same quantity, and that her weight was stable.

As Jennifer was fixing the tubes Roger arrived to double-check that everything was working satisfactorily. It seemed these days that the children knew that his first consideration was Wendy, because they watched what he did and stared wide-eyed at the large machine with its many attachments.

Roger was unbelievably gentle in dealing with her, then he took her small hands in his.

'I do believe those little warts are getting smaller and smaller, don't you think so, Wendy?'

She nodded and smiled. 'Jenfer rubs leaves on them, and they'll go away one day soon.'

'And every day this machine is going to make *you* get better, we hope,' said Roger.

He joined Jennifer, and as they were walking away he remarked,

'Good news about Robin—Orthopaedics are pleased with the result and say he can be discharged and come back daily for physiotherapy.'

'Daily? That's going to be awkward for his mother. I believe there are other children at home,' said Jennifer.

'I was wondering about that. Get the social services to have a word with his mother and find out the circumstances. Maybe he'll need to stay in for a while longer, so we won't raise his hopes just yet.'

Robin lurched drunkenly towards him and grabbed him around his thighs.

'Are my legs better now?' He looked up with enormous brown eyes.

Roger swung him up into the air. 'They look pretty good to me. Maybe they'll need to get a bit stronger before you go home. What do you think?'

'I want to stay here with you and Jenfer. I like it here.' He staggered to his locker and took out the drawing of himself that Roger had given him. He looked at it and laughed aloud.

'I look funny. I don't really look funny, do I?'

Roger smiled. 'Do I?'

'Yes,' gurgled Robin. 'You look very, very funny.'

'Then that makes two of us,' Roger replied. 'We can laugh at each other.'

He stopped beside the bed of the little girl who

had had a tonsillectomy the previous day.

'Has there been any excessive bleeding?' he asked Jennifer as he read the notes.

'No, she's doing very well.'

'No earache?'

'No.'

'Good.' He replaced the notes and squatted down beside the bed. 'Those nasty lumps have gone now, what do you think about that?'

Her mouth turned down and her eyes filled with tears.

'Let me have a peep, sweetheart.'

'It hurts,' she whimpered.

'Let me see, then.' She opened her mouth for him to examine it. 'Mm, yes, it's sore, isn't it? I know what we'll do, we'll give you some ice-cream. Would you like that?'

She nodded damply and gave a wobbly smile.

Roger patted her shoulder. 'Okay. Just hang on until I've spoken to the other children, then you shall have some.'

As they walked away Jennifer said, 'Promises, promises! The freezer has packed up. The engineers are working at it, but there's no ice-cream.'

He looked as disappointed as a small boy who had been deprived of a treat, and Jennifer smiled. Seeing the smile, he frowned.

'It's not a laughing matter. I promised Jane some ice-cream and she's jolly well going to have some!'

Jennifer looked at him challengingly. 'And how

do you propose to arrange that? Bunny-get-you-better hasn't got any on her trolley, I can promise you that.'

'So Fairy Red Pencil will have to pop out and buy some. That'll take the smile off your face.' He fished in his pocket and took out some coins. 'Have some yourself while you're about it.'

'But—but I don't know where any shops are, and I can't just go out like that, without permission,' she protested.

Roger looked like a large, firm rock. 'Without permission? *I'm* giving you permission. It's doctor's orders.'

'But—but where can I get it?'

'You'll find somewhere. Oh, there's a news-agents along the street. They sell sweets, so perhaps they've got ice-cream.'

'What shall I buy?'

'Get a block and it will do for them all. We can't have the other kids clamouring to have their tonsils out.'

With a carefree feeling as if she'd been given an unexpected holiday from school Jennifer left the hospital behind her. The sun was shining and this afternoon she was off duty, and Roger had remembered the party when he'd called her Fairy Red Pencil. Everything was lovely.

Roger was a kind man. But why shouldn't he be? He had everything going for him. Quite obviously he came from a privileged background and could cock a snook at protocol and rules. He was the one with authority, he could do as he liked, dress as he wished. As far as she could see all this would make for a stormy relationship between him and Sarah, because she appeared to be someone who would demand her own way. However, it was possibly the novelty of having someone to dominate her that appealed to her.

After several abortive attempts Jennifer found a shop which sold ice-cream. She gave a wry smile at her feeling of triumph, for she was the one who had vowed never to touch the stuff again! When she got back to the ward Roger was still in there, sitting on a bed with children milling around him. At Exmouth sitting on a bed was very much frowned on, even if it was just one person perched on the edge, she couldn't imagine what would have been said about an onslaught such as this.

'Eureka!' she announced, handing him the block of ice-cream and his change. 'I got the biggest one I could. Was that right?'

'Yes, thanks, that's fine.' He looked dubiously at the block and at the expectant children. 'They're going to get into one hell of a mess, and that means more work for you,' he added apologetically.

She smiled. 'No, it doesn't. It's my afternoon off and any mess will have to be dealt with by Debbie. But there won't be any. I'll fetch some saucers and spoons and a knife so that you can divide it up, please.'

Jennifer took Jane her ice-cream first and Roger dished out the rest for the others, then joined Jennifer holding a saucer of ice-cream in his hand. As she put a spoonful in Jane's mouth he tapped Jennifer on the shoulder. She looked around.

'Open wide,' he said, and fed a spoonful to her.

But the gesture he meant so kindly was the worst thing he could have done, for those words 'Open wide' brought Simon vividly to mind. When she had swallowed the mouthful she shook her head.

'No more, thanks.'

'No more? Don't you like ice-cream?'

'Not really.'

'Have some more,' he coaxed. 'If I give this extra to any child I'll be accused of favouritism, and that won't do. Come on now.'

He placed an ice-cold hand on her chin and as she gasped he took the opportunity of putting another spoonful in her mouth.

Choking, she protested, 'Don't you ever take no for an answer?'

'Not if I can help it,' he replied cheerfully. 'And now I must love you and leave you—I've got work to do.'

Roger moved away, then paused and came back. 'You said you had the afternoon off. Are you doing anything special?'

She hesitated. If he was going to invite her out

would she have the strength to refuse?

'No, not really,' she said, and waited, her foolish heart thudding.

'Then I suggest you go to Windsor Castle, it's Garter Day and is something I think you'd like to see.'

'Garter Day? What's that?' she queried.

'You must certainly go. The Queen and members of the Royal Family walk in a procession from St George's Hall to a service in St George's Chapel. It's at half past two, but you need to get there early.'

'Why Garter?' she asked.

'It's held nearly every year, for the Knights of the Order of the Garter—the King or Queen, as the case may be, awards the Order to people of outstanding achievement—it's the highest order they can be given. There are only twenty-five altogether, including members of the Royal Family.'

'How often is it held?'

'Annually now, though it stopped for a while after Edward the Third founded it. It was George the Sixth who celebrated the six-hundredth anniversary of the inauguration and it's been held almost every year since. But you can get a programme at the Castle and it'll tell you more about it than I can.'

'I'm sure it's very spectacular. I may go along, then.' Jennifer was ashamed to realise that she was disappointed that he didn't propose to go too.

Roger chuckled. 'You have to apply for tickets months beforehand.'

She raised her shoulders. 'So what's the point of telling me to go?'

He fumbled in several pockets and drew out an envelope which had lost its pristine freshness.

'You can use mine, because I can't go.'

She smiled warmly. 'Well, thank you, that's kind of you.'

'There's just one thing.' He took out the impressive-looking card and pointed to the name on it. 'It's made out to Dr Grant, so as far as anyone is concerned that's who you are. Don't forget, or you won't be allowed in.'

Jennifer's mouth dropped open. 'Me? Dr Grant?'

''Fraid so.'

'But what if someone collapses and a doctor is called for and they pick on me?'

'Then you use your initiative. You know what to do if someone collapses, so do it.' He laughed and strode away, leaving her staring at the ticket with mixed feelings.

But by the time she had taken up her position near St George's Hall she had overcome her trepidation. The sky was a cloudless blue, the sight of hundreds of visitors wearing colourful clothes and the picturesque setting of Windsor Castle filled her with pride that this was her country and she would soon be seeing the Queen. The Royal Standard flying high over the Castle fluttered gently in the breeze and there was the sound of bands playing in the distance.

According to her programme there would be the Knights Companions and the Officers of the Order and the Officers of Arms in the procession, and here they were. It made a wonderful sight, Guards in red uniforms with medals and decorations, wearing bearskins or shining helmets. There was a roar of applause as the Queen Mother came into sight, and Jennifer found herself clapping too. The Queen and the Duke of Edinburgh were wearing dark mantles and plumed hats, but Jennifer found it impossible to identify who everybody was, but that didn't matter at all. The Queen had earlier invested the new Knights Companion of the Order of the Garter and now they were on their way to the Chapel for the installation service.

When the Queen had passed, the crowd hurried, half running, jostling each other, hoping to reach the Chapel before she did and so be able to see her at close quarters again. From within the Chapel came the sound of organ music and when the Queen arrived at the West Door there was a fanfare of trumpets. Then the doors closed after her and the crowd dispersed, to throng the streets of Windsor.

Jennifer wandered around looking in shop windows and stopping outside the Theatre Royal to read the posters. She'd heard that the Royal Family frequently patronised the shows and that it was a delightful theatre. Some time she must visit it if she could get Debbie to go too. Windsor was an unusually attractive town with some cobbled streets and the Castle and the vast number of tourists who gave it a high-class holiday atmosphere. There were numerous pleasant cafés, and Jennifer decided to have tea.

She saw to her amusement that on the menu various herbal teas were available, but she settled for straightforward Indian. She ordered cream cakes, although she knew she shouldn't, but they looked delicious with strawberries nestling in cream in meringue cases. She was eating one, slowly savouring every morsel, when someone said,

'Do you mind if I sit here?'

Jennifer looked up at the perfect profile and saw that it was Sarah Betts. She smiled a welcome.

'Hello, do you remember me? We met at Mrs Constable's for a Sunday lunch.'

Sarah's eyes travelled coolly over her before she gave a small smile.

'So we did. It's Jocelyn, isn't it?' She drew out a chair.

'Nearly right—it's Jennifer, actually. Isn't it a lovely day?'

Sarah glanced at the cream cake Jennifer had on her plate, then somewhat disapprovingly at her figure before ordering lemon tea and nothing to eat.

'That's what I should have had, but I'm a pig where cream cakes are concerned. Still, I don't have them very often,' Jennifer said.

'Are you still on holiday?' Sarah was looking at the passers-by as if she wasn't very interested in her reply.

'Oh no, thanks to Dr Constable I'm working now.'

Sarah looked at her then, her thin eyebrows arched. 'Dr Constable? Why? What are you doing?'

'I'm nursing in the local hospital,' Jennifer told her.'

'So you're a nurse? Dr Grant is at that hospital, but you wouldn't come into contact with him. He's in charge of the children's department.'

Jennifer smiled. 'Oh yes, I work in that ward. He's awfully good with the children.'

A shadow crossed Sarah's eyes. 'He won't be there very much longer,' she said.

Jennifer felt a tug at her heart-strings. 'Won't he?'

'No. He's with Dr Constable this afternoon, that's why I'm free.'

Jennifer left the remaining crumbs of her meringue, for her appetite had gone. 'Is he thinking of working with him?'

Sarah looked thoughtful as if this were a new and possible idea.

'I don't think he's considered that. No, it's to do with him starting a practice of his own in Harley Street. He doesn't want to be stuck in the NHS.'

To break the silence that ensued Jennifer asked with an effort,

'Do you work in Harley Street all the time?'

'Oh no. Dr Constable visits three hospitals and I accompany him to take his notes, etcetera.'

'That sounds like a nice job, and interesting too. Especially as I should think Dr Constable was a pleasant man to work for.'

'Mm, yes. But it will be better when Roger has his own practice and we can work together.'

Jennifer didn't want to continue that conversation, so to change the subject she said,

'I went to Windsor Castle this afternoon to see the Garter procession, it was very impressive. You've seen it, of course?'

'No, as a matter of fact I haven't. I was free this afternoon, but I believe you have to apply for a ticket ages beforehand. When did you get yours?'

'This morning,' laughed Jennifer. 'Dr Grant gave it to me because he couldn't use it. That must have been because he was seeing Dr Constable.'

Sarah looked at her coldly. 'He gave it to you? But he knew *I* was free.'

Jennifer had spoken unthinkingly, but now wished quite desperately that she hadn't.

'He—he gave it to me on the spur of the moment. He—he probably thought he couldn't get it to you in time.'

'Nonsense—we lunched together.' There was a hard gleam in Sarah's eyes as she prepared to leave, her chin held high. 'No doubt he believed I'd seen it many times before.'

'Yes, I'm sure that's right,' Jennifer agreed. 'It's nice to have seen you.'

But it hadn't been nice. In fact it had ruined Jennifer's afternoon. Not only had she been made to feel guilty and greedy at eating a cream cake and being given the ticket by Roger, but that snippet of news that he had been going to leave the hospital had left her devastated. How the children would miss him—and not only the children. For to know that he was in the building and might put in an appearance at any moment gave the hospital a warmth and feeling of well-being.

So he was going into private practice, and Harley Street at that. He had such charisma that it was only right he should reach the top of the tree, but what a loss he would be to the hospital. When he moved to London would he still wear his sloppy clothes and bow tie, or would he conform to what his wealthy patients would expect? Would he wear a smart suit and a buttonhole? That picture of him made her feel inordinately depressed, because it would be the end of the Roger she knew and admired. The large, untidy, clumsy, lovable character would have vanished.

CHAPTER SIX

JENNIFER had a few days' leave. In other circumstances she would have gone home to Exmouth, but it was too soon to face her parents and her friends. So she made a couple of trips to the London stores, managed to get a solitary returned ticket for the matinee of a popular musical and visited Madame Tussauds. She had enjoyed the break, but as her holiday drew to an end she found herself thinking more and more about the hospital, the patients and—well, she could admit it to herself —Roger. One evening she went to a local pub with Bernard, but it was an occasion she preferred to forget. Everything that poor man said seemed to tie her up in embarrassed knots, although she supposed he meant well and she was continually vowing she would try to be nicer to him.

But it was with a feeling of happy anticipation that she returned to St Anselm's. Rose stopped her on the way to the ward and called her into her office. Jennifer's spirits fell. Was this it? Was she going to tell her that her temporary post was at an end?

'Hello, my dear, have you had a good holiday?'

'Well, it was a break, but I can't say I'm sorry to

be back.' Jennifer eyed her warily.

'So you find you like working with children? I remember you weren't sure about that.'

'Oh yes, it's super, I like it better than anything else. You know, it's so rewarding to see the kids going home as fit as fleas when they've been so poorly.'

'Yes.' Rose didn't sound as happy as usual, and Jennifer waited uncomfortably to hear what else she was going to say. 'Unfortunately that isn't always the outcome.'

Jennifer stared at her. 'What are you trying to tell me, Rose?'

'It shouldn't be difficult, but we've all become so fond of her. The fact is Wendy isn't responding to dialysis as well as we'd hoped, so she needs to spend more and more time on it, which of course is a hopeless outcome for her future, unless she can have a transplant.'

'Do you think she'll get one?'

'Roger has had her kidneys typed and particulars have been sent everywhere, but——' Rose shook her head, 'nothing suitable has come up as yet.'

'And she hasn't any brothers or sisters, has she?'

'No. Both parents have offered their kidneys, and tests are being made to see if they're suitable.'

'If they are that'll be the answer, won't it?'

'Well, we'll have to see. In the meantime Wendy is staying on the machine most of the time.'

Jennifer nodded unhappily. 'It's a shame. Has Robin gone home yet?'

'Robin? Yes, he went yesterday. The physio says twice-weekly sessions should be sufficient now and his mother can manage to bring him in then, so we'll see how he gets on.'

'We'll miss him,' said Jennifer. 'Roger will especially. Any new admissions?'

'Yes, I was going to tell you about John. He's nine years old and was admitted with severe convulsions.'

'Epilepsy?'

'No. Apparently he had a mild attack of bronchitis and his mother gave him some junior aspirin. A few days later he started these convulsions, which were so severe that he had to be tied to the bed. Then late that night he went into a coma. Fortunately Roger had stayed on because he was worried about his condition.'

'I bet he was! So what happened?'

'Roger rang a specialist friend in Harley Street and asked for advice.'

Jennifer looked shocked. 'Asked advice? I'm surprised he didn't have an ambulance take him to a London children's hospital right away.'

'He wasn't in a fit state to be moved, so Roger wanted this confirmation of his own opinion as to treatment,' explained Rose.

'So what then?'

'He's in the special care unit on a life support

machine and is being drip-fed. Apparently he's suffering from Reye's Syndrome owing to the aspirin. Actually they've withdrawn it from the market now.'

'I didn't know it could cause that. Oh, heavens!' exclaimed Jennifer. 'I very nearly told someone to give junior aspirin to a little boy who'd fallen in the river and was suffering from shock. I can't think what stopped me, except that I was a bit shocked myself. What a blessing!'

Rose shook her head. 'Aspirin doesn't cause Reye's Syndrome, it just acts as a trigger to the virus which has already got into the system.'

'I see. So how is he doing?'

'He's still in a coma, and his parents take it in turn to sit with him around the clock and they play tapes made by his school friends to try and rouse him. We can only hope for a miracle.'

Rose and Jennifer stared at one another, each thinking how tragic it was that such a simple thing as a junior aspirin could prove to be so dangerous.

'So all this happened while I was away, and it was only five days,' Jennifer remarked.

'There you are then, you mustn't go on leave again,' said Rose with a smile.

'But you know, I was afraid you were going to say it was curtains for me.' Jennifer looked anxiously at her.

'And the way they're cutting down I suppose anyone of us could be given our marching orders.

We can only live one day at a time. Oh, another child was brought in with pains in the appendix area and we're waiting to see if it settles down.'

'Boy or girl?'

Rose smiled. 'A boy, called Roger. As you can imagine, that gives our Roger scope for a bit of fun!'

'He's so good with the children. It would be a great loss if he left,' Jennifer said to test Rose's reaction, to see if she had heard anything.

'But he's very clever and talented and probably has his sights set higher. And that's only right.'

'Mm, that depends on what motivates him. If it's money, then yes, he should move on. But I doubt if he'd get such job satisfaction elsewhere.'

Jennifer hadn't realised that the door behind her was ajar and Roger was about to come in.

'Who wouldn't get such job satisfaction elsewhere?' he asked, as if he had the right to know.

Rose raised her eyebrows. 'That's a saucy question, Roger. We were discussing a hypothetical case.'

'So that's what you do when you should be in with the children, Jennifer,' he said cheerfully. He reached out and grasped her firmly by the shoulder. 'Come along now. When you get two women together they forget everything if they're having a good gossip.' He turned and winked at Rose.

'Rose was telling me about Wendy,' Jennifer said. 'Have you any further news?'

Roger leaned against the wall by the ward doors. He nodded.

'Her father isn't a suitable donor, unfortunately.'

She looked up into his worried brown eyes. 'What about her mother?'

'We're waiting to hear.'

'So there's still hope for her?'

'There's always hope,' he said angrily, then his anger evaporated. 'I'm a bit worried about her mother.'

'But why? People can manage quite well with only one kidney, can't they?'

'Certainly.' He looked at her with a faint smile. 'You don't know if you've got two kidneys and I don't know if I have.'

'So why are you worried?'

'It's her general state of health. She's a frail lady who's had major surgery recently, and I'd rather the father could have been the donor.' He stared thoughtfully into space, then brightened up. 'She'll cope all right,' he said cheerfully, then walked breezily into the ward, as if he had cast aside a cloak of depression.

'Roger!' the children all called.

He didn't reply, but looked across at a remarkably healthy-looking little boy.

'Well, aren't you going to answer them?' he demanded.

The boy grinned. 'They mean you,' he said.

Roger pointed to himself with a massive forefinger. 'Me? I'm Dr Grant, they wouldn't call me Roger, would you, children?'

'Yes, Roger,' they chanted, and fell about laughing.

He examined the boy so gently his hands barely seemed to touch him, and yet he appeared satisfied. 'Do you know what I think, Roger? I think you've been having us on.'

'I haven't, I haven't!' the little boy shouted.

'You haven't? Well, with a bit of luck it may settle down.'

Roger fished in his pocket and took out a ten-penny piece, examined it, then put it back and took out another.

'This is the lucky one. You keep that and wish on it and we'll see what happens. Right?'

He left Wendy until last, and Jennifer could sense his reluctance to go to her.

'How's my girl?' he asked gently.

She could scarcely smile, but she tried. Roger read her chart and took her wrist to feel her pulse. Then he held her hand.

'Those little warts are disappearing, aren't they?'

Wendy glanced at them unhappily.

'They're not going quickly enough for your liking, eh? That's because Jennifer's been away, but she's back now to rub some more pennywort on them.' He glanced questioningly at Jennifer and she nodded.

'Yes, my mother sent me some more and they arrived this morning—lovely fat juicy ones.'

'Good. Did you hear that, Wendy?'

When he had gone, as always the ward seemed empty. But Bunny-get-you-better wheeled in her trolley.

'Hello, Debbie,' smiled Jennifer.'

'Hi, Jennifer, did you have a good time?'

'I suppose so, but it's good to be back.'

Debbie with her tall Bunny ears looked surprised. 'I bet your boy-friend was glad to see more of you.'

'My boy-friend?' Jennifer looked at her blankly, then remembered. 'Oh, you mean Bernard. I don't know if he was pleased or not.'

Jennifer took a doggie eggcup to small Roger and watched while he drank the medicine. When she returned to the trolley Debbie remarked,

'You don't seem all that keen on Bernard.'

'Don't I?' Jennifer tried to summon up some enthusiasm. 'I expect it's because I'm shy and don't like to show my feelings.'

'If he was my boy-friend I'd show my feelings all right!'

'You would?' Jennifer eyed her with surprise.

'Not 'arf! He's super-looking—he's got everything.'

'We-ell, I suppose I'm biased,' Jennifer said with difficulty. But she knew that if she gave Debbie the slightest indication that Bernard was only her cousin the news would be around the hospital in next to no time. Having Bernard as a makebelieve boy-friend was hard to swallow, but he acted as a safety valve, if anyone was interested they would know she wasn't free. And she didn't intend to be free ever again.

Jennifer was about to go off duty when she heard that the boy with Reye's Syndrome was still in coma; the boy with a possible inflamed appendix was flushed and whimpered with pain, so Rose sent for Roger.

Jennifer stayed on to hear what he had to say. He came in breezily, like a breath of fresh air.

'Debbie—Jennifer, these will buck you up.' He handed them a ticket each. 'They're for Thursday night of next week at the Royal. Don't get too excited, Jennifer,' he added. 'When they give us complimentary tickets it usually means they aren't doing very well because it's a dud show. Isn't that right, Debbie?'

'I don't mind about that, it's an evening out and I'll enjoy it whatever it's like,' Debbie said happily.

Roger went first of all to Wendy to check her pulse and blood pressure, then looked at her chart to see that her fluid input and output were roughly the same. Then he smiled and patted her shoulder before going across to Roger.

'Hello, old man,' he said to his namesake. 'What's this I hear about you having a bit of a tummyache?' As he spoke he was taking Roger's pulse. Then he gently felt the area around his appendix. 'I'm going to ask a friend of mine to have a look at you. Okay? You know what they say, two heads are better than one.' He winked at the boy and moved away.

'Ben will probably operate tonight, unless it'll keep until tomorrow,' he said. 'I'll hang on and see. Are you off duty, Jennifer?'

'Yes. Unless you need me.'

'Need you?' His warm brown eyes rested on her for a moment and she felt the colour flood her cheeks.

'I—I mean I'll stay on if required,' she said stiffly.

'I know what you meant,' he said. 'But Sandra and what's-er-name from the agency will be coming on duty soon, Rose says.'

Jennifer walked home wondering who what's-er-name was and hoping very much that Roger would never refer to her in that casual manner.

Aunt Marian and Bernard were watching the television when she arrived home. As usual Bernard was complaining about the programme.

'They put on such a load of rubbish,' he said, turning his back on it.

'Oh well, sometimes people pay good money to see rubbish,' said Jennifer. 'We've been given tickets for the show that's on at the Royal and Roger says when we get them it usually means the play isn't going too well.'

Bernard gave her his surprised look. 'Are you going to use the ticket?'

'Yes. An evening at the theatre is nothing to be sneezed at. Besides, people's ideas of what makes a good play differ. I might think it's terrific.'

'Beauty is in the eye of the beholder, eh, old girl? You don't need to tell yours truly that.' Bernard gave a little laugh. 'As a matter of fact I was looking at the posters today and rather liked what I saw. Some good-lookers in the cast, believe you me! Maybe I'll cast an eye on it myself.' He gave a self-satisfied smirk. 'Cast—cast—get it?'

Jennifer smiled weakly. 'Ours is certainly a strange language. It must be difficult for foreigners to learn, though they seem to manage.'

He looked at her expectantly. 'I hope you'll ask me to join up with you all. That Sarah——' He raised his eyebrows.

'I can't do that,' Jennifer said hastily. 'The tickets are numbered and we've got a block for our staff —well, I suppose we have,' she added doubtfully. 'Sorry about that.'

Then she wondered. Would Roger be there, and if so, who would be sitting beside him?

CHAPTER SEVEN

JENNIFER could feel the happiness in the atmosphere as she went on duty. Rose was singing 'It's a lovely day tomorrow', but Jennifer believed it was going to be a lovely day today.

'Shall we make it a duet, or are you quite happy singing solo?' she asked, putting her head around the office door.

Rose laughed. 'I didn't realise I was singing aloud or I might have had second thoughts—singing isn't my strong point!'

'Never mind, it shows you're feeling happy, and no wonder—tonight we go on the razzle, don't we? And I've heard it's a jolly good play, despite our doubts.'

'The play?' Rose gave a start of surprise. 'I'd forgotten about that.'

'You've forgotten? Oh, I see, you're one of these people who makes theatregoing a regular event. Not like me, when it's a real thrill. So why are you singing? What are you auditioning for?' grinned Jennifer.

Rose shook her head and hugged herself as if she'd just won an unexpected first prize for something. 'No, it's more wonderful than anything like that. John has come out of his coma and he's going to be all right!'

'Oh, isn't that great!' Jennifer clasped her hands together.

Rose nodded. 'It's on occasions like this that you realise that nursing is the most satisfying job in the world. Nothing else could give you that glow of absolute joy as knowing that somebody who was desperately ill can suddenly take a turn for the better. Especially when it's a child.' She gave an embarrassed smile. 'In our job we can see miracles.'

Jennifer allowed them both some moments of joyous thought before asking, tentatively, if there were further developments in Wendy's case.

The light in Rose's eyes faded and was followed by a shadow of doubt. 'Well, yes, her mother's kidney is suitable for transplant and she's anxious to donate it, so I believe the operation will go ahead, because Wendy's condition is deteriorating. But they're waiting as long as they safely can in the hope that another kidney might turn up.'

'Because of her mother's state of health?' asked Jennifer.

Rose nodded. 'That's right. Personally I think they're being over-cautious.' Then she shrugged. 'But who am I to say? The surgeons know the history and they don't want either of them dying on them.'

'Poor little girl! I've become very fond of Wendy,

and I'm sure Roger has too. The trouble is I feel so helpless. The only thing I can do is to rub pennywort on her hands, and that's so unimportant, but it gives her some pleasure.'

'It certainly does, and the warts don't seem so bad now. Is it that stuff working, do you think? Or normal healing?'

Jennifer shook her head. 'I've been talking to Wendy while I've been rubbing it on, and I've been so touched by her little pale face and huge wistful eyes that to tell you the truth I haven't noticed if the warts are fading or not. I must have a look at them.'

She went to her locker and took out a juicy leaf of pennywort and smilingly approached Wendy's bed.

'Hello, darling,' she said, while her heart gave a pang of dismay at seeing how frail the child looked. 'How are our little warts doing?' She felt pleased surprise that they had noticeably diminished in size and were now scarcely more than dots. She rubbed the leaf carefully over each one. 'They've almost gone, haven't they?'

A faint smile appeared in Wendy's eyes and she gave the suspicion of a nod.

Jennifer wished she could recall some cure of her grandmother's that would help Wendy's kidneys to function properly, but despite Roger's teasing remarks she knew that her granny was no witch who dabbled in magic potions but just a countrywoman who had faith in the things that grew in the hedgerows, and there didn't seem to be one for kidneys.

As Jennifer did her daily round of giving medicines, making beds, washing the small patients,
taking temperatures and pulses and blood
pressures when necessary, checking and changing
drips and all the while talking cheerily to the children, there was still a part of her mind which was
devoted to her own affairs, and on this occasion it
was Bernard who occupied her thoughts. For despite her intense dislike of his mannerisms, the
things he said and his self-satisfaction, a small part
of her felt deeply sorry for him. He was the victim
of a too-adoring, possessive mother. Everyone who
knew her described her as a 'honey', sweetness
itself, but Jennifer had the feeling that the loving
admiration she showered on Bernard could be an
unconscious ploy to keep him with her, to escape
the lonely future she might have had when her
husband died. Not unnaturally Bernard basked in
her admiration and believed that he was the 'heart-
throb' she insisted he was, having heard it so often.
But despite his boasts of all the 'little ladies' he
could have if he as much as snapped his fingers
Jennifer had seen no evidence to support his claim.
However, although he was a bore, she had at times
made use of his company, knowing there would be
no sexual advances from him for her to parry. But
making use of him made her feel guilty.

What was on her mind today was the knowledge
that he would have loved to have gone to the
theatre with them tonight, and she felt as if she had

excluded a child from a party. He led a lonely life, despite the occasional outings with his mother and the learner drivers he encountered daily. But after spending an hour in his company she believed that even the most eager man-hunter would realise he was a bore and that they'd be wasting their time. As she saw it he was destined to have a lonely future, and she was sorry, but there was no way she could include him in the outing tonight.

'Jennifer,' Debbie asked that afternoon as they were turning a mattress, 'would you mind if I went off a bit early?'

'Like when?'

'Like now,' Debbie said hopefully.

'No, I don't mind, but it isn't up to me, you'll have to ask Rose. Don't tell me you're going to spend all this extra time making yourself look beautiful for tonight?'

'No, it's for tomorrow night. I need a perm badly and this afternoon is the only time the hairdresser could fit me in.'

'Oho! So what's on tomorrow night?' asked Jennifer with a smile.

Debbie's eyes sparkled. 'I've got a date with a staff nurse on Men's Medical. He's really got what it takes. I'm certain he's going to end up as an SNO. He's called Rodney. The nurses joke about that and pronounce it Rodannay, but I think it's lovely. They're just jealous.'

'I look forward to meeting him. He must be

something if he's got you to have a perm—you've been saying you need one ever since I came here,' Jennifer laughed.

'Well, there isn't much incentive when your hair is hidden under your cap all the time. But tomorrow he's taking me to a dance, so I want to look my best.'

'So who's a lucky girl, having two dates in one week? I'm lucky to have any at all,' laughed Jennifer.

The door opened and Debbie hurried across. 'There's Rose. I'll tell her you don't mind if I go now. See you later. What time shall we get to the theatre?'

'It says quarter to eight on the ticket, but I'll be there before half past seven. I like to look around,' said Jennifer.

The children were settled. They'd been given their supper. Some of them were able to feed themselves, but others needed to be fed spoonful by spoonful, which took longer than usual tonight because Debbie wasn't there. However, when she could find the time Rose came in and lent a hand, and at last all was ready. The older children were reading and the younger ones tucked up in bed. The telephone in Rose's office sounded stridently, and after a few moments she came hurrying into the ward.

'There's an outbreak of food poisoning in some children who've been to a party this afternoon.

We'll need extra beds set up. Oh dear, and Debbie has gone off. Never mind, we'll have to do the best we can before night staff come on duty. I'll ring the porters to bring the beds and you pop along to Roger's room and try and catch him before he leaves.'

Jennifer sped along the corridor and pressed the button for a lift. It took so long to arrive that she was tempted to run up the stairs, but at last it zoomed down and the doors slid open and out stepped Roger.

'Just the man I'm looking for,' said Jennifer. 'A number of children have arrived in Casualty suffering from food poisoning and some will need to stay overnight at least. Rose asked me to tell you.'

'Of course, I'm glad you caught me. Are any of them in the ward yet?'

'No, the porters have got to put up the beds first. Rose has contacted them.'

When the children arrived they were crying, vomiting and having diarrhoea, and dealing with them was a non-stop job. The noise disturbed the other children, who also demanded attention. The night staff arrived, but even so they were all kept busy.

At last Roger glanced at his watch, then laid his hand on Jennifer's shoulder.

'It's time you were leaving or you'll miss the first act. Off you go!'

Jennifer looked at him with bemused eyes, as

she comforted a small boy, and mopped up his vomit.

'First act? Oh, the theatre—I'd completely forgotten. What's the time?'

'It's just on seven. Another nurse can finish off here.'

'But what about you? You're supposed to be going to the theatre too,' she reminded him.

He moved quickly to the bedside of a child who was crying and obviously in some pain.

'I shan't be going,' he told her.

Another patient urged and tried to vomit again. Jennifer persuaded him to sip some boiled water, then realised that he had soiled the bed. He sobbed loudly, bitterly ashamed of the accident.

'Don't you worry, pet, there's nothing at all to be upset about. I'll clean it all up in a minute. Don't cry, my love.'

As she went to the linen room for fresh sheets she knew she couldn't just leave, when all available help was so badly needed. It was such a pity, because she'd really been looking forward to going to the theatre and her ticket would be wasted. Suddenly she thought of Bernard and hurried to Rose's office, picked up the telephone and dialled his number.

'Bernard,' she said hurriedly, when he answered, 'if you'd like to go to the theatre tonight you can have my ticket—I'm tied up here with an emergency. Do you want it?'

His voice, which was always slow, seemed slower than ever.

'You're tied up with an emergency?' he drawled. 'That's a good one, old girl. What's he like, this emergency? He wouldn't be called Roger, by any chance, would he?'

'If you want the ticket you can pick it up at the porter's desk in the main hall. The show starts at a quarter to eight.' Jennifer slammed down the receiver.

Puffing with irritation, she returned to the ward, not thinking now about her missed outing but enjoying her work and the feeling that she was doing something useful. Eventually most of the children's symptoms subsided and there was an uneasy silence in the ward, broken occasionally by a whimper or a cry.

'I think we day staff can go now.' Rose looked around the crowded ward until she saw the night Sister. 'We're off now, Eve,' she called.

'Yes, of course. Thank you all for staying on, it was good of you.'

Roger looked from Rose to Jennifer. 'You haven't used your theatre tickets,' he realised.

'Actually I gave mine to Muriel—you know, she's in charge of kitchen staff. She's a nice kind soul and she'll enjoy it, I'm sure,' said Rose.

Roger looked at Jennifer, and she flushed. 'I—I offered mine to Bernard on the phone. I hope you didn't mind my using your office one, but I did it to save time.'

'Of course. What about you, Roger?' asked Rose. 'Wasted, I suppose?'

He shook his head. 'I wasn't going anyway. I gave mine to Sarah.'

'Didn't you fancy going?'

'It wasn't that, but I've got an important appointment tomorrow afternoon and I must do some work on it beforehand.'

'And you haven't been able to get it done? That's a shame.'

'I've got the rest of the night to do it in while you two are sleeping your pretty heads off. I know you live in, Rose. But what about you, Jennifer? Can you get home all right?'

'Yes, thanks, I'll be fine. I don't live far away. Good night.' She smiled at them both.

Jennifer went home via the theatre. The lights shone and there was an occasional burst of laughter which she could plainly hear. She stood, pretending to study the posters. She would have liked to have been in there, but a small part of her felt glad that after all Bernard would have an evening out.

CHAPTER EIGHT

'So WHAT was the play like?' Jennifer asked Debbie the next morning.

'Hold on a sec. It's time for Bunny-get-you-better to make her entrance.'

Debbie whisked out of the ward, to return shortly afterwards wearing her rabbit's ears and tail and pushing the decorated trolley. They wheeled it slowly around the ward, checking each patient's requirements, but there was little the children needed in the way of medication.

'I mustn't forget to do my bit with the pennywort,' said Jennifer. 'Wendy's warts have practically disappeared and she's so pleased. Poor little soul, I do wish she could get well and strong.'

'Hi, Kevin, don't do that!' Debbie, convulsed with laughter, retrieved a sticky eggcup from a small boy's head where he was wearing it upturned like a hat. 'Did you drink the medicine first?' she asked him.

'Yes,' he said, bright-eyed.

'I don't believe he did,' Debbie told Jennifer when she rejoined her. 'His hair was as sticky as a punk's.'

'Perhaps that was the idea,' Jennifer suggested.

'But do tell me about the play.'

'Oh yes. Well, it was quite good—I've seen better—but I enjoyed myself. There was a nice little group of us and we had coffee in the interval. Pity you couldn't make it in the end. The kids seem to have recovered. I suppose they'll be going out this morning.'

'Roger said he'd given his ticket to Sarah. Was she there?'

'Yes, she was there in all her glory, and sitting next to your boy-friend. You want to watch him —he was making up to her something chronic.'

'That must have been nice for them both,' Jennifer said drily.

'Sarah always looks out of this world, doesn't she? She was wearing a scarlet silky sort of crêpe dress, very tight-fitting, and she had a marcasite brooch on her shoulder and ear-rings to match.'

Jennifer felt a sudden pang, as she wondered whether Roger ever called *her* Fairy Red Pencil when he saw her wearing it.

'So she and Bernard seemed to get on well together, did they?' she remarked.

'I think so. I know he's good-looking but, I say, he's pleased with himself, isn't he!' Debbie clapped her hands over her mouth. 'Sorry, I forgot I was speaking about the man you love.'

'Be my guest,' shrugged Jennifer, wishing she could tell Debbie the truth about their relationship.

Rose came into the ward to check the condition of the children who had had food poisoning.

'Did they find out what caused it?' asked Jennifer.

'Yes, apparently it was the cream in the cakes. It was a mild outbreak, but with children you can't be too careful. Most of them are quite all right now, but I want to have a word with Roger about Hazel, that child in the end bed.'

As if on cue Roger came in. None of the children yelled a greeting or ran to meet him today, for many of his patients had left and the new ones hadn't yet got to know him.

'How are they today?' he asked, glancing around the ward.

'They seem all right except for Hazel Drew over there. She's dehydrated. She probably ate more cream cakes than the others.'

'Right you are, I'll take a look.'

He endorsed Rose's diagnosis and ordered a saline and glucose drip. For once he seemed withdrawn as if he had something on his mind. Rose looked at him questioningly. His velvety brown eyes had a faraway expression and he seemed to be staring into space. Then, as if he had physically thrown a blanket of despair aside, he said,

'I hear that last night's play wasn't too brilliant, so you didn't miss a lot.'

'Now I don't know who you heard that from,' Rose said aggressively. 'But Muriel, who had my ticket, can't stop talking about it. She said she had a smashing time.'

Roger smiled. 'One pro and one con. What did your boy-friend think of it, Jennifer?'

She felt herself blush scarlet. She would never feel reconciled to having Bernard referred to as her boy-friend. 'I've no idea,' she replied.

He eyed her for a moment or two as if about to say something more, but changed his mind and turned away.

There was something very dull and quiet about the ward today. Nobody was crying or fighting over toys. Nobody was talking or laughing, and Jennifer, who was sometimes overwhelmed by the noise, missed it. She wouldn't like it to be always so quiet, it depressed her.

As Roger was leaving the ward he laid his massive hand on her shoulder and swung her around to face him.

'You're feeling low and so am I. I'm going to visit Eastleigh Children's Home this afternoon. Would you like to come too for the ride?'

Jennifer thought she would rather do that than anything. Then she remembered Sarah's displeasure when she heard that Roger had given her his ticket for the Garter ceremony, and she hesitated.

'Shouldn't you invite Sarah?' she asked.

He frowned, his thick dark eyebrows meeting in the middle of his forehead.

'Why?' he demanded.

'Well—she is your girl-friend . . .' Her voice died away.

He placed his other hand on her, thus imprisoning her. His eyes seemed to be studying her as if she was a specimen under a microscope.

'My dear good girl, I'm inviting you to have a run out in my car because you missed your theatre outing last night and seem fed up. I'm not suggesting that you go to bed with me.'

At those words a thrill ran through her body, and she didn't want him to remove his hands from her, but he did.

She raised her chin and looked at him defiantly. 'Thank goodness for that! Actually I would have enjoyed the outing, but I'm on duty.'

He dragged her towards Rose. 'This nurse of yours is very much on edge and obviously depressed, so I offered to take her with me to Eastleigh this afternoon. She worked several hours overtime last night, so I take it she can have this afternoon off?'

'Oh yes,' Rose said warmly. 'The run will do her good. Nice thinking, Roger.'

He turned to Jennifer. 'See you in the car park, then, at half past one. I can't wait for you.'

He had taken it for granted that she wouldn't refuse, and he was right. To drive out into the countryside was a treat she felt she needed.

They arrived in the car park at the same time.

'Good girl,' smiled Roger. 'Hop in.'

To her surprise he wasn't dressed casually, but wore an immaculate white shirt under a dark blazer.

'You're looking very smart,' Jennifer told him.

'Yes, aren't I?' he said, glancing down at himself. 'I've got to set a good example.'

'Who to? Me?' She had thought she too was looking rather smart in a cream suit and a brown blouse, but of course there was always Sarah as a yardstick with whom to compare herself.

'You? Why should I set you a good example? You always look very nice. I'm talking about the kids at the Home.'

The trees had shed most of their leaves, but those that were left were colourful against the clear sky. In the hedges hips and haws glowed red amongst the dark green foliage. Autumn was Jennifer's favourite season.

'Are you the Home's doctor?' she asked.

'No. I go there from time to time to try and discharge a debt. You see, I was brought up there.'

'You were? You mean your father was the Superintendent?'

'No, I don't mean that. I've no idea who or what he was. I had a mother who left me in the ladies' cloakroom at Harrods in one of their carrier bags.'

Jennifer couldn't have been more surprised.

'Why? I mean, did she ever come forward?'

'No. She left a note written on expensive notepaper saying she had to remain anonymous, that her family knew nothing about me. She said I was to be called Roger. I've still got that note. It's all I have got from my parents.'

Jennifer laid her hand impulsively on his arm. 'Oh, how awful! But when you were adopted, were you happy?'

Roger looked across at her with an enigmatic expression. 'I wasn't adopted. As you can imagine, I was a very large and noisy baby, and people who want to adopt usually go for cute baby girls who smile and gurgle.'

'Do you mean you lived in the Home all the time?'

He nodded. 'They fostered me out several times, but I always ran away and went back there. It was my home, and the people who lived and worked there were my family.'

Jennifer's belief that he had come from a privileged background was knocked sideways. She was hopeless at forming correct opinions, she thought.

'So how did you get your name?' she asked.

'I was Roger Harrod when I was here,' he told her.

They entered a tree-lined drive and stopped outside a large white building which looked as if it could once have been a stately home.

'Here we are—Eastleigh Children's Home.' He got out of the car and stood looking at the building and at the garden for several moments.

He turned to Jennifer with a smile. 'This was my home. Those were the trees I climbed,' he said simply, then turned and lifted a large cardboard box from the back seat of the car.

Jennifer put out her hand to detain him as he started to walk towards the entrance.

'So why are you called Grant?' she asked.

'If you want to know more you'd better come into the hall. But you'd probably prefer to wander around the countryside, so here are my car keys in case you get back first.'

'Oh no,' she said, refusing them. 'I'd like to hear what you have to say.'

The hall was filled with boys and girls of all ages, and Jennifer tried to picture Roger as one of them, without success. She sat on a chair at the back of the hall with teachers and house mothers, while the Superintendent introduced Roger to the children.

Jennifer listened with interest and pride as Roger told them amusing anecdotes of his early days in the Home.

'I was happy here,' he said. 'I had security, comfort, companionship and care—loving care. What more could anyone wish for?' He looked slowly around the rows of upturned faces before continuing.

'And if any of you feel, as I suppose we all do at times, that we've been short-changed in life, that we haven't the same chances as if we had a mother and father and family, I want to dispel that idea, once and for all. I was found in a plastic carrier bag and after a few weeks brought here. Now I'm a doctor, a paediatrician—which means I'm a children's doctor. And I'm in charge of the children's department in St Anselm's hospital. It's a good job, an excellent one, and I couldn't feel happier or more fulfilled in any work. I got where I am, not because of a privileged background or wealthy parents but because of the encouragement and help I was given here. It wasn't easy, but I worked hard, took exams and went to university and later to medical school on a grant—that's how I chose my name, Roger Grant. Because of that I'm constantly reminded of all I owe to Eastleigh. Now I'm not setting myself up as someone who's done wonders, I'm not boasting, but I'm proud, and I want you all to know that what I did any of you can do. Maybe you wouldn't want to become a doctor, but that's beside the point. Whatever your choice, go for it with everything you've got. Be determined to get there and you will. If you're a road sweeper make your area somewhere to be proud of, because it's better to be an excellent road sweeper than an unsuccessful, unhappy doctor. And never forget the debt you owe to this Home where the loving care and encouragement is second to none. I'm proud to have been brought up at Eastleigh Children's Home. Are you?'

There was a roar as the children shouted 'Yes!' and cheered and clapped.

When Roger sat down the Superintendent took his place. After thanking Roger for coming to speak to them he told the children that a special tea had been laid out for them in the dining room.

'And just a moment, children,' he said, removing the lid of the cardboard carton which Roger had brought in. He took out a large, elaborately decorated iced cake, which was greeted with cries of delight.

'Three cheers for Dr Grant,' he said. 'Hip, hip——'

In the dining room the children, with wedges of cake in their hands and their mouths full, thronged around Roger, eager to ask him questions. He was obviously in his element and answered them sincerely and at some length, so that Jennifer wondered whether they would ever be able to leave. But at last he was free.

When they were driving home, she said, 'That was an excellent speech you made, Roger.'

He looked pleased. 'Was it? Do you think it went down all right with the kids?'

'You know it did,' she replied, somewhat amused because he seemed to be wanting praise. 'Mind you, I can't see many of them being as successful as you are.'

'I don't see why not. If I did it then they can.'

'But don't you think some of your success could be because of inherited traits from your mother's family?'

'My mother's family? Why?' he demanded.

'Because it seemed she was from a well-to-do family. Her father was probably——'

'Wealthy and proud and unforgiving. I don't want to inherit any of those characteristics. I want to do what I can to help people, especially children. If I earn a good living doing that, it's a bonus. But money for its own sake means nothing to me.'

Men! What frauds they were. Here he was talking like this while at the same time he was making arrangements to practise in Harley Street. And what would that be but working for money amongst wealthy people? Of course he inherited traits from his family, including that of pursuing girls until he'd had his fun and then dropping them. For wasn't that what his father had done?

CHAPTER NINE

AT DINNER that night Jennifer asked Bernard what he thought of the play.

'I've had mixed opinions, and I'd like to know what yours is,' she explained.

He gave her his faintly surprised look, then grimaced.

'It was very third rate. The chap in it—I don't remember his name—was very amateurish. Seemed to be looking towards the prompt a lot of the time as if he'd forgotten his lines.'

'Poor man, that must be an awful feeling. But what about the play itself? Did you think that was good?'

Bernard piled more vegetables on his plate, then looked at her and his mother with raised eyebrows, 'I haven't taken too many, have I? Is that all right?'

'Yes, Bernard, you eat up, it will do you good,' his mother said. Then, as an afterthought, 'Oh, have you had enough, Jennifer?'

This was a daily ritual which never failed to irritate Jennifer. Bernard ate for a few minutes, and she watched as he shovelled large forkfuls of food into his mouth before continuing the conversation.

'The play? So so. But I'm afraid I've got some bad news for you, old girl.'

'Bad news? For me?'

He smiled into his steak and kidney pie. 'Who do you think sat beside me? Sarah Betts! And I must say it made quite an occasion for both of us.'

Jennifer stared at him, fascinated, but could say nothing.

'She's a real good-looker, just my type. So I'm afraid you've lost me, old girl. It's a case of pastures new from now on.'

His mother clicked her tongue. 'I'm sure you don't mean to be unkind to Jennifer, but you mustn't forget what she's been through,' she chided.

'What?' He looked vaguely from his mother to Jennifer. 'Oh, you mean the wedding—oh yes, of course.'

Jennifer felt everything inside her shrivel with dislike and shame. Dislike of his terrible conceit and shame because of their oblique reference to her 'wedding day'. Until now they had maintained a studied silence on that subject. Her tensed nerves were beginning to relax, when Bernard said, with a sound that was something between a chuckle and a snigger,

'I'd like to be a fly on the wall when Roger Grant hears I've pinched his girl!'

It was too much! 'You'll only be saving him the bother of dropping her,' said Jennifer sharply.

He gave her a glassy stare. 'Dropping her?'

'You said that Roger has a reputation for dropping his girl-friends when he's had his fun,' she reminded him.

'That? oh—ha, ha—surely you didn't take me seriously?'

'But that's what you said, and you weren't joking.'

'But that was simple tactics. A successful lover has got to get rid of the opposition. Tactics, old girl, tactics. Get my meaning?' Bernard pushed his empty plate away and leaning back looked at her through half-closed eyes.

'But if it wasn't true then what you said was libellous!' she said furiously, knowing how it had affected her thoughts of Roger.

'Ah,' he said, smoothing his moustache, 'you're wrong, there, old girl. The word you were looking for was slanderous. There is a difference, you know.'

'Slanderous, libellous—what it was, was lies, all lies!' she fumed.

'Now then you, two children, stop squabbling,' Aunt Marian said mildly.

Jennifer forced herself to eat some pudding which she didn't want, because she knew that otherwise she would be thought to be sulking. But as soon as she was able she went to her room. She didn't know how long she could stand living here, but if she were to get a room somewhere else her father would be very hurt, for he and Marian were the only members of their family who were left and they were devoted to each other. She appreciated her aunt's hospitality and knew that both she and Bernard intended to be kind. It was just that they irritated her, and she wondered whether perhaps she irritated them, and feared that could be so.

Winter replaced autumn overnight. Jennifer awoke to hear the whistle of the wind and rain spattering on the window and to feel that her nose was cold. At breakfast Bernard offered to drive her to the hospital, and it was occasional moments of thoughtfulness like this that made her feel guilty.

On arrival at the hospital she felt a great sense of relief to be here where she loved to be. But as she was about to go into the ward Rose called her into her office. She was seated at her desk with a pile of papers in front of her.

'Sit down, Jennifer,' she said, and Jennifer did so with a sense of foreboding.

'Have you had any luck in applying for other jobs?' Rose asked.

Jennifer's heart sank. 'No, I must confess I haven't applied for anything yet.'

'But you knew this was purely temporary, didn't you?'

'Yes, I know, both Dr Constable and the SNO told me. But I'm so happy here I couldn't bring myself to apply for anything else. You don't mean——?' She looked anxiously at Rose.

'Oh no, no, I haven't heard a thing, but the six months will soon be up and you really should be looking for something else.'

Jennifer's mouth felt dry. 'I know I should. But I really hate the thought of leaving. This is such a happy hospital, especially our ward.'

Rose nodded. 'It is indeed, and you've fitted in very well. We won't want to lose you, you know.'

Jennifer stared unhappily at the carpet. 'There's no chance of a permanency here, I suppose?'

'That's not for me to say, Jennifer. But I do know that the nurse you're replacing is due to return here at the end of January.'

'So I'll have to be out by then, I suppose?'

'I'm afraid so. While you're here I'd like to get the holiday rota fixed. I've put you down to have Christmas off, I'm sure you'll be pleased about that.'

Jennifer felt as if a cold hand had squeezed her heart at the thought of returning to Exmouth, but as she had leave she would have to go there.

'That was sweet of you, but I honestly don't mind working if someone else would like the time off,' she said hopefully.

Rose pursed her lips. 'The alternative would be for you to have New Year off, and if you'd moved on by then you'd have forfeited it.'

'What a horrible start to a New Year!' Jennifer clenched and unclenched her fists.

'Well, it's on the cards, isn't it?'

'I bet it's nice here at Christmas time.'

'We make it as festive as we can, but we send as many home as possible, and those who stay aren't all that well, so I'm inclined to find it rather a sad time,' said Rose.

The weeks sped by quickly, there were many things Jennifer found to do. She helped Aunt Marian choose Christmas presents and cards as well as buying her own. She helped make decorations for the ward. They would be put up during Christmas Eve. Her mother phoned several times and was delighted that she would be spending Christmas at home.

She felt a reluctant sadness for Bernard who had nothing much to look forward to, apart from large helpings of turkey, for any outings he might have visualised with Sarah had come to nothing.

Roger had been on leave, but Jennifer had no means of knowing whether he and Sarah had spent it together.

It was the day before Christmas Eve and Jennifer was catching the afternoon train home. Now that it was nearer the time she had a childish feeling of excitement mixed with dread. Christmas was always fun—well, it had been. She had enjoyed the church service, meeting friends, seeing cards on the mat, opening presents and over-eating. This year it would be different, for she couldn't go to that church again, it would bring back such dreadful memories. Never mind, she would stay at home and see to the dinner, leaving her mother free to go to the service if she felt so inclined. With luck, none of her friends need know she was home.

Her heart lifted as Roger came into the ward, large and gorgeous, wearing a wide bow tie in emerald green with ladybirds on it. She gazed at it fascinated. Where *had* he got it?

He greeted Jennifer with a smile. 'It's too early to wish you a happy Christmas, too soon to kiss you under the mistletoe, but you wait, my girl, until Christmas Day.'

'I won't be here,' she told him regretfully.

'You won't?'

'No. I'm going home today.'

'Going home, she tells me casually, not caring that she's spoilt my Christmas!' he laughed, laying a massive hand on her shoulder. 'Never mind, I'm an unselfish sort of bloke, and I hope you have a good time.'

'Thank you, I hope you do too,' she replied, feeling bereft.

He walked away, then came back 'Wendy and her mother are having their ops after Christmas, on the Wednesday,' he told her.

'That's the day I come back. I do hope all goes well.'

'It isn't a perfect match, but we'll keep our

fingers crossed—and a special Christmas prayer wouldn't come amiss.'

'I'll remember,' Jennifer said softly.

Her father was at Exeter station to meet her. It was great to see him again, she just wished she wasn't so very sensitive, for she felt he looked at her just that second too long as if wondering if she showed any signs of stress or embarrassment. Of course she felt both, and again when she kissed her mother, who held her for that extra moment. Would she never recover from her traumatic experience? Would she remember it for the rest of her life?

'I haven't bought any holly yet!' her mother said the following morning. 'I meant to get it yesterday, but it was raining cats and dogs, so I left it.'

'That's OK, we'll have all the cards to put up —and haven't we got some decorations stowed away in the loft?'

'No, I threw them out last year because I thought we'd be——' Her mother ended there, embarrassed because she'd been going to say 'I thought we'd be spending it with you in your own home'.

They glanced sheepishly at each other, then her mother said, falsely, 'I thought we'd be getting some new ones, those were shabby.'

'Well, I'll go out and buy some greenery if you like,' said Jennifer, anxious now to get away from this atmosphere which was heavy with unspoken knowledge.

It was a cold morning with an unexpected hint of frost in the air. Jennifer was fond of Exmouth, it was a small town with a good variety of shops that looked festive with turkeys and geese and piles of tangerines made to look gay with an occasional one wrapped in silver paper. Windows were hung with blobs of cottonwool on string to emulate the snow which seldom fell at Christmas, yet had always seemed to be a part of that season.

She wandered around the market enjoying the atmosphere. She bought some crystallised ginger which her father liked and some brazil nuts coated with marzipan which were a favourite with her mother. She looked at the attractive crackers, but decided they were really for parties or children. Her thoughts went back to her ward. This was about the time of day Roger would arrive. A tiny thought sneaked into her mind. Would he have kissed her under the mistletoe? She shrugged. If he had it would have meant nothing, because there was Sarah. But just to have felt the joy of him holding her so close, his large arms around her —She turned sharply aside in an effort to send her foolish thoughts flying, and instead she almost knocked an old lady off her feet and sent her handbag to the ground. She apologised profusely, and someone picked up her handbag and passed it to her. Jennifer smiled and thanked the person. Her smile faded, for she was looking straight into Simon's face. They both stood for a moment as if petrified, then they began to move away from one another. The lights from the stalls shone on his glasses so she couldn't see the expression in his eyes, but his normally pale face had flushed red.

'Oh, hello—on holiday?' he asked, turning back. His voice was thin and sounded strained.

'Yes.' She cleared her throat. 'And you?'

'No, I've just got the day off for Christmas shopping.'

He was tall, but somehow, in Jennifer's eyes, he seemed to look skimpy and he stooped a little. She had always thought that was rather endearing, that it made him look scholarly, but now it made him look weak. Wasn't he going to mention their 'wedding day'? Wasn't he going to give her some explanation? Apologise for leaving her standing there? He wasn't. He was about to walk away when she stopped him.

'I believe I should congratulate you,' she said, looking hard at him.

He tilted his head and suddenly she could see the startled expression in his eyes.

'Oh, you mean——'

'You're married to Sheila Mailer, aren't you?'

'Yes—er—thank you. And I'm afraid she's waiting for me, so I must dash.' He slithered away like an eel.

As Jennifer watched him go all her feelings of rejection went with him, and for the first time since that dreadful day she felt free. She smiled widely.

What a miss, what a lucky miss! Fancy being stuck with a man like him for life! Goodbye, Simon, and good riddance, she whispered.

She bought some holly which was laden with red berries and decided to walk along the sea-front. She stood looking out at the wide expanse of water and breathed in the salty sea air. This was the end of the past. Tomorrow she would go to church and greet any friends who happened to be there. And she would give thanks to God for what had happened.

It would be a long time, if ever, before she could recover from the psychological wound and forget the shame and embarrassment of that awful day, but she believed that the way to speed that recovery was not to hide away but to put on a brave face. She told herself that she must always remember that there is nothing either good or bad but thinking makes it so.

CHAPTER TEN

By the time Jennifer returned to the hospital the Christmas decorations had been taken down and all that remained was one shrunken balloon which had been overlooked and hung from a ceiling fitment, wrinkled and colourless.

Childishly Jennifer had hurried on tiptoe past Rose's door in case she heard her and called her in to tell her that her job there was over. She had applied for two vacancies without success and she couldn't pretend to be sorry, for a geriatric ward in a London hospital or a men's surgical in the Midlands were not to her liking.

Debbie was changing a bandage on a small boy's leg. As always she looked happy and wholesome, with her frizzy dark hair, rosy cheeks and infectious smile. Jennifer knew how much she would miss her when she had to leave.

'Hello, Debbie, did you have a good Christmas?'

'Hi, Jennifer, so you're back. Yes, it was very nice. I've got two bits of news for you,' Debbie added excited.

Jennifer laughed. 'Let's hear it, then—I'm all agog!'

'Well, there was an article in *Woman's Own*

or *Woman*—I'm not sure which—all about Roger!'

'Roger? Why, what's he done?' Jennifer passed her a clean bandage from the trolley.

'It was about him having been brought up in an orphanage. I tell you, I was amazed! I always thought he was an eccentric aristocrat! I wonder what Lady Sarah thought about that? I wonder if he'd told her?'

'She should admire him for that, but being Sarah——' Jennifer shrugged. 'Did you keep a copy of the magazine? I'd like to see it.'

Debbie shook her head. 'No. It wasn't mine anyway, it was just being passed around. Don't you want to hear my second bit of news?'

'Of course. Let's hear it, and it had better be good,' said Jennifer.

Debbie's eyes twinkled. 'I've got a ring!'

'Oh, Debbie, I *am* pleased. So your Rodney has come up to scratch?'

Debbie chuckled. 'I knew I'd fool you! No, the ring was a lucky charm in the Christmas pud, which I nearly swallowed. Some luck!'

'It would probably have passed through you and as it was supposed to be lucky you might have retrieved it,' Jennifer laughed. 'But talking of rings, how goes your love life?'

Debbie wrinkled her nose. 'What love life? If you mean Rodney it's non-existent. There's no other girl involved, my rival is his work. He's completely dedicated and ambitious, and I don't think I could live with that.'

'Then don't even think of it—for a girl like you, who likes her bit of fun and games, it would be hell.'

'It's all very well for you to talk, you've got your bloke.'

'I have?' asked Jennifer, wide-eyed.

'Bernard, of course,' said Debbie.

'Oh—Bernard.' Her voice was dismissive, more so than she even realised.

'I don't know, I'm sure, I just can't understand you,' said Debbie. 'He's got everything, and you never seem all that thrilled about him. You love him, don't you?'

The very suggestion horrified Jennifer, but she knew she must keep up her pretence or there would be too much embarrassing explaining to do.

'Let's say I hide my feelings,' she replied, and felt she'd been rather clever.

'And what true feelings are they?'

She heard and recognised the voice behind her and turned slowly to savour the moment of seeing Roger after what seemed ages. He looked even more appealing than he had in her thoughts. His hair was thicker and glossier, his eyes darker and more gentle. She glanced instinctively to see which bow tie he was wearing. It was the blue one with red spots, the one he had been wearing on her first day here. He saw her glance at it and put up his hand to touch it.

'For luck,' he said softly.

'Luck?' she queried.

He nodded. 'Wendy and her mother are having their transplants today.'

'So they're going ahead with it? I thought they were going to wait as long as they could?' said Jennifer.

'Yes—well, this is obviously the moment they think is right, but it's a difficult decision to have to make. I'm thankful I'm not a surgeon.'

'Hasn't surgery ever appealed to you?'

Roger shook his head vehemently. 'No, not at all. I don't even like giving injections, so I wouldn't be much good, I'm afraid.'

'How's your needlework?' she asked laughingly, meaning suturing.

'Rotten.'

'Then tell me who sewed those ladybirds on your other tie?'

He seemed pleased. 'So you noticed them? Believe it or not, I put them on with my own fair hands.'

'But you've just said you can't sew,' Jennifer protested.

'And I'm not one to lie,' he smiled. 'You see, it had big red spots on it and that was that. Then as I was walking through the grounds a ladybird landed on me and I thought one of the spots had fallen off. But no, it was a real live one. So I took my pen and drew some spots on the spots and hey presto, I'd got a ladybird tie.'

Jennifer laughed. 'You're just a kid! I bet you enjoyed doing that.'

He nodded. 'And the kids like them. One little girl drew away from me and yelled. She thought they were real.'

'Did you have a good Christmas?' asked Jennifer.

'It was on the quiet side, but Mrs Constable very kindly invited us there on Boxing Day, and I enjoyed that.'

Us. Him and Sarah, of course. Did she realise how very fortunate she was?

After a few moments Roger asked, 'Did your boy-friend go to Devon with you?'

Once again she felt revolted. 'I went alone,' she said shortly.

'That was a shame, but you had a good time?'

'Thank you, yes.'

Jennifer wondered what he would make of it if she told him that while she had been home she had laid a ghost.

'The ward seems very quiet today, and I don't like it. Goodness knows I don't want any child to be ill, but I miss—it's a funny word to use—but I miss the liveliness of the children yelling and fighting over some toy and staggering around.'

'You should have been a nursery schoolteacher instead of a nurse if that's what you enjoy,' Roger said thoughtfully.

'Oh no!' she hastened to contradict him. 'I love nursing really.'

He nodded. 'I know. Have you attended to the little girl with her arm in a sling?' He glanced across to where a small dark-haired child lay listlessly on her bed.

'No, I haven't had time yet. What's her trouble?'

'She's got a greenstick fracture of the humerus.'

'How did that happen? Did she fall out of a tree or something?'

He raised his eyebrows and there was a cynical expression on his face.

'Her mother said she'd fallen downstairs.'

Jennifer looked at him sharply. 'And you don't believe that?'

He shrugged. 'I suppose she *could* be one of these people who are prone to accidents and who bruise easily.'

'Well, if you fell downstairs I should have thought you could bruise yourself very badly.' She looked at him, puzzled.

'Mm. X-rays show other untreated injuries—ribs, her arms and a leg. I suppose it's possible they were accidental.'

'You think someone caused her injuries? What's her mother like?'

'I haven't seen her yet, but Rose said she didn't seem the type, she was a slight, timid lady. It could be a husband or boy-friend.'

'Or rough children at school?'

'Could be. I'm going to have a word with their GP when I can get hold of him, see what he has to say about the family. There's nothing else we can do. The rest is up to the social services.'

Jenny felt flattered that he should be confiding his opinions. It wasn't the usual way with doctors, who often treated a nurse as if she was of no consequence. But as always Roger was a law unto himself, and did just what he wanted to do.

They walked across to the little girl's bed.

'Hello, Heather,' Roger said gently.

To Jennifer's shocked amazement she cowered away from him, something no other child had ever done. He and Jennifer exchanged a glance, both thinking that it was probably a man who ill-treated her—if anyone did.

'How are you feeling, love?' asked Jennifer gently. 'Looking forward to Mummy and Daddy coming to see you, aren't you?'

A look of fear came into her eyes. 'No, no,' she whimpered.

'Would you remove the sling, please, Nurse, I'd like to examine her arm.'

Jennifer removed the sling and turned back her sleeve to reveal a discoloured swelling.

'Oh dear, what *have* you done?' she asked.

To her surprise Heather said, as if she was reciting something she had learned by heart,

'I tripped over my slipper and fell down the stairs. It was my own fault.'

'Was it now? That was a nasty accident, wasn't
it?'

'It's true, it's true!' the child insisted hysterically,
as Roger gently felt the bones in her arm.

'All right, my dear, you'll have to be more
careful in future, won't you? Thank you,
Nurse, you can replace the sling.' He walked
away.

Heather seemed to relax when Roger had gone,
and Jennifer wondered why.

She chatted to the child, then asked her if she had
any brothers or sisters.

'We've got a baby. He cries all the time,' said
Heather.

Jennifer had a picture in her mind of the home
conditions. A sickly harassed mother, a crying
baby, a high-rise flat on the umpteenth floor and a
father who was either a drunkard or frustrated in
some way—probably both.

But when it was visiting time she believed that, as
usual, she'd been wrong in her opinion, for they
seemed concerned about the little girl and brought
her fruit and sweets and fancy biscuits. Jennifer
watched them from a distance and saw Heather
looking at them nervously, but she seemed no more
scared of her father than her mother. And when
they were leaving she clung to her father as if she
didn't want him to leave. So did the mother do any
battering? But if she did, why had Heather been so
scared of Roger?

It was much later that Roger came back into the ward and went up to Rose. Seeing them talking together and the eager expression on his face made Jennifer edge nearer to them to hear if they were talking about Wendy and if there was any news. Roger saw her and nodded with a wide smile. He raised his thumb in the air.

'The op's over,' he said delightedly.

'I'm so glad. So everything went all right?' she asked unnecessarily.

'Yes, it went splendidly. They're both in special care, so we must keep our fingers crossed.'

Jennifer's heart swelled with pure joy, not only for Wendy but for Roger, who was so obviously relieved and delighted.

Rose looked at her uncomfortably. 'I'm sorry to spoil this moment, Jennifer, but there's a letter for you in my office,' she said.

Jennifer's smile vanished. 'Oh no!' she exclaimed.

'I'm sorry, my dear.'

'May I fetch it, please?'

'Of cour——No, I should leave it until you're going off duty,' Rose advised kindly.

Roger looked from one to the other of them. 'What's all this? Obscene letters?' he asked cheerfully.

'You could say that,' Jennifer replied bitterly.

Rose gave a wry smile. 'It's certainly one way of putting it.'

He searched her face, even in silence seeming to demand an answer.

'It—it's my job here. I was warned it was only temporary, and now——' She shrugged unhappily. 'And now it's come to an end.'

'So you'll be leaving us?'

Jennifer couldn't trust herself to reply, so she merely nodded. Roger put his hand on her shoulder and she could scarcely stop herself from bursting into tears, but she held her breath and tensed her jaw, and the moment passed.

'Are you fixed up anywhere else?' he asked.

'No,' she said flippantly. 'Nobody wants my services, but I daresay I'll survive.'

He stood a moment longer, and slowly looked her up and down. Then he nodded.

'Well, good luck anyway,' he said, and walked away.

The day seemed to go downhill from then on. Jennifer wondered how much notice they would have given her and how soon she would be returning to Exmouth to apply for any vacancies that might be going. She was going to hate leaving Rose and Debbie, but it was just as well she would be leaving Roger. For despite her determination never to become emotionally involved with another man, let alone a man who was attached to another girl, it was becoming increasingly difficult. Indeed, she had to admit to herself that she had lost that particular battle, the only consolation being that Roger would never guess.

When at last she was off duty she went reluctantly to Rose's office to collect her letter. Rose pretended to be rummaging in a cupboard for something, and spoke over her shoulder.

'Your letter's on my desk. Help yourself, dear.'

Jennifer picked up the crisp white envelope with her name neatly typed on the front. She held it for a moment, undecided whether to open it here or wait until she reached home. Rose turned and looked at her compassionately, and it was that look which made up her mind.

'Well, here goes,' she said, and tore it open.

Her eyes blurred at first, but when they cleared she saw that it was not an official letter but a very friendly one from Dr Constable. A smile spread across her face.

'It isn't my notice, Rose. It's from Dr Constable.'

'Dr Constable?' Rose was clearly puzzled.

'Yes, he says that one of his staff nurses is leaving and as this is only a temporary job here, he wonders if I would be interested in working for him. He suggests that I go up there some time this month to have a look around his nursing home.'

Jennifer and Rose stared at each other thoughtfully. 'In private practice. How do you feel about that?' asked Rose.

'I'm not sure. I mean, it's such a relief that this isn't the letter I was afraid it was, although Dr Constable clearly thinks I'll soon get the push. But

Harley Street and private practice!' Jennifer shook her head. 'I don't think that's really me, but on the other hand he's awfully nice, and I've nowhere else lined up. What's your opinion?'

Rose leaned her chin on her hands. 'I know what you're saying and I'm inclined to agree with you about private practice. But there's no harm in you looking around, because it *is* a job, and it's in pleasant surroundings. You might find you liked it very much. Even if you didn't it wouldn't be a life sentence, you could leave when you wanted to.'

Jennifer had listened thoughtfully. 'That's an idea.' She looked wistful. 'I wouldn't consider going there if there was any possibility of my staying on here. But I suppose——' The sentence trailed away.

'I think you should put that out of your mind, dear. You go up to Harley Street and have a look round some time.'

'Thanks, Rose, I'll do that.'

'You'd better ring and make an appointment beforehand,' Rose suggested.

Jennifer nodded. 'Yes, of course. But that does make it all sound so dreadfully final.'

Rose patted her hand. 'Life can't stand still, you know. You run along home and count your blessings.'

CHAPTER ELEVEN

WHEN ROGER had finished his ward round he drew Jennifer aside. It was moments such as these that she knew she would miss so very much. She looked questioningly into his velvety eyes.

'I want you to do something for me,' he said, with an air of pent-up excitement, almost like a child on Christmas Eve.

'Certainly. What is it?'

He seemed to be hugging some lovely secret to himself.

'Wendy is improving by leaps and bounds, she'll be coming back into the ward and sitting out in the next day or two,' he told her.

'That's wonderful news. What about her mother?'

'She's doing fine too—she went into the general ward yesterday. Now what I'd like you to do is this. When next you're off duty would you buy a pretty little dress for Wendy, please?'

'A dress? She has some in her cupboard, I think.'

'I daresay, but you being a girl yourself, you'd know that something new to wear gives you a boost. I'm sure it would please her. Get her a blue one.' Roger fished in his pocket and took some notes from a clip and handed them to her. 'If it comes to more than that let me know.'

Jennifer's eyes were dark with fond admiration. 'That's so thoughtful of you. And yes, you're right, she'd love that. It would probably do her a world of good too.'

He looked pleased. 'Can you spare the time?'

'Of course I can.'

'Good.' He squeezed her arm. 'Oh—don't broadcast it, or all the kids will want something new.'

Jennifer laughed. 'And I'm certainly not willing to shop around for the lot of them!'

When he had gone she went to see how Heather was doing. She had certainly suffered a number of untreated injuries, and Jennifer and Rose were still trying to discover whether they had been deliberately inflicted or were the result of accidents. The fact that she was so timid led them to believe the former—and yet the parents seemed caring and generous. In her cupboard hung pretty clothes and her locker was full of books and toys.

'Hello, Heather, your arm is mending nicely, so I expect you'll be going home soon. That'll be nice, won't it?'

Heather stared at her unsmilingly.

Jennifer said, 'You'll see your baby brother. What's his name?'

'Peter. He cries all the time.' She seemed about to cry herself.

Jennifer put her arm around her. 'You mustn't worry about that. Babies do cry a lot, it doesn't mean they're unhappy, it's to stretch their lungs and help them to grow healthy.'

'Mummy doesn't think so.'

'I expect she's worried in case he's got a pain in his tummy.'

Heather looked with wide blank eyes at Jennifer. 'Mummy screams and screams and says it's my fault.'

'Your fault? She doesn't mean that. How could it be your fault?'

Heather shook her head.

'You wouldn't hurt him, would you?' said Jennifer gently.

'I threw him on the floor.'

Jennifer managed to restrain her start of surprise and said calmly,

'Why did you do that?'

'I wanted to hold him like Mummy does, but I dropped him.'

'But that's an accident—to let him fall is very different from throwing him on the floor.'

'He banged his head on the stool and there was blood all over his forehead. He screamed, and Mummy came in and said I'd done it because I was jealous.' Heather burst into tears.

'That was because she was so worried at seeing the blood, and Peter lying on the floor,' Jennifer explained. 'Of course she doesn't really think you did it deliberately. Children are always banging themselves—look at all the bruises you've got! My goodness, how did you get those?'

'Mummy hit me——' The little girl stopped, her eyes full of fear.

Jennifer held her breath, then said gently, 'What did Mummy do?'

'No, no, she didn't do anything. I tripped over my slipper and fell downstairs—Mummy said so.'

'Of course, you told me that before, didn't you? All right, love, everyone has to be careful on the stairs. It's easy to fall. Now would you like some orange juice?'

Jennifer knew that to have persisted in her questioning would only have upset the child, and she believed she now knew enough. The mother was worried about the baby and rightly or wrongly blamed Heather, and when he cried she vented her anxiety and anger on her, by hitting out at her. Possibly the father knew nothing of it. Jennifer thought she had cleverly worked it out. It was later that she remembered Heather's fear of Roger, and wondered why.

She went into Rose's room to tell her of the conversation.

'Good, that gives us a clearer picture,' said Rose. 'I'll pass on the info to the social worker.'

Jennifer nodded. 'What do you think of the father? Heather seemed so scared of Roger, of all people, and there surely must be a reason.'

'Who knows? The social worker will no doubt ferret that out. Quite possibly it's a violent household and the father, being the biggest and strongest, would instil in her the most fear. It's out of our hands, my dear. We can only deal with the injuries and inform the proper people.'

It gave Jennifer immense pleasure to go shopping for Wendy's dress. She went to several shops just for the joy of looking through the stock, before selecting a cornflower blue dress with a white yoke embroidered with small red flowers which delighted her. It was expensive, but Jennifer was certain Roger would approve her choice.

She called in for tea at one of the many pleasant little restaurants in Windsor. For a heady few minutes she pretended to herself that the dress she had bought was for her and Roger's daughter. Then she came back to earth. She knew she was foolish, that Roger wasn't interested in her, but in Sarah, and that she was building up for herself eventual withdrawal symptoms, but the knowledge failed to stop her. Telling herself that he was a philanderer at heart, the same as other men, didn't help either, for now that she knew him better she didn't believe that, especially since Bernard admitted that he'd lied about him. Indeed, if Roger had any faults they were so outweighed by his virtues that they were of no significance.

The following morning Jennifer took Wendy into a side room, where she dressed her in the new frock. It was hard to believe that this was the same child who had been so pale and listless, for she was almost as lively as any other child of her age.

She laughed with delight at her new dress, then held up her hands to Jennifer. 'Look, all gone,' she said, referring to her warts.

'Well, aren't you the lucky one,' smiled Jennifer. 'And soon you'll be going home and then back to school. My, that's a funny face! Don't you like school?'

'Now that my hands are better I don't mind,' Wendy confided.

Roger came hurrying into the ward as if afraid he would miss curtain up at a play. He beamed his approval and winked at Wendy.

'My, my! You're going to make some lucky young man a very pretty wife one day,' he told her.

She slipped her hand in his. 'You. I want to marry you, Roger,' she said, smiling up at him and tossing her plait over her shoulder.

'Marry me? We'll have to see about that. My young lady might not approve, but we'll keep our fingers crossed, eh?'

He looked at Jennifer with a conspiratorial wink, but a vision of Sarah came between them and she couldn't return his smile.

'Wendy, why don't you go and speak to that little girl over there?' she said. 'She's called Heather and she'd like to know you.'

Wendy tripped happily across the ward and soon

the two little girls were talking and laughing together.

It was several days later that Jennifer kept her appointment in Harley Street. It was a cold, wintry day and the pavements not unduly crowded. She wrapped her scarf tighter around her neck. As she looked up at the leaden sky a snowflake fell on to her eyelashes and she shivered.

It had been bad news at the hospital. When Jennifer went on duty she had been distressed to see that Wendy was back on dialysis.

'Why? What's happened?' she asked Rose.

The Sister frowned. 'Her temperature soared during the night and she's showing signs of rejection. So she's on increased doses of the anti-rejection drugs and is on dialysis to be on the safe side.'

'Is that usual? Will she be all right?'

'Unfortunately it happens sometimes. We hope she'll pick up, but she might have to stay on dialysis until another transplant is available. So you're off to Harley Street now?'

'Yes. I'll just have a word with Wendy before I go.'

Jennifer held the little girl's hands. 'Never mind, my love, you'll be better in a day or two, you'll see,' she said. But her heart was heavy as she left.

She checked the numbers on the expensive-looking doors, then rang the bell to the clinic. For the first time she realised that she might see Sarah here, and didn't relish the thought. But it was an older woman, very elegant and well-spoken, who summoned a nurse to show Jennifer around.

'I'm Emma Griffiths,' the nurse said. She had a serious face and her hair was brushed away from her ears. 'We have six rooms that are occupied at the moment, but I'll show you one that's free. They're all the same except for the colour scheme. They're very attractive, I think.'

She opened the door to a room decorated in turquoise blue. There were floor-length satin curtains and a fitted carpet.

'There's an en-suite bathroom for each room,' she said, and Jennifer glimpsed the turquoise bath and wash-basin.

'How lovely,' she said. 'It would certainly make being ill very pleasant. Have you worked here long?'

'About eighteen months, and I'll be leaving soon.'

Jennifer looked at her questioningly. 'So if I came here would it be your job I was taking?'

'That's right. You know there's a flat that goes with the job, don't you?'

'A flat?' A wave of delight shot through Jennifer at the prospect of not having to look for accommodation. 'No, I didn't know.'

'Well, I'll show it to you. It's more of a flatlet, but jolly convenient, and it saves not only time but fares and rent.'

It was a large L-shaped room, divided by sliding screens to form a living room and a bedroom; there was a small kitchen and a bathroom, and plenty of cupboards.

'It's fantastic! How can you bear to leave it?' asked Jennifer.

'With difficulty,' Nurse Griffiths smiled. 'But I've got a pretty good exchange. I'm marrying a Scot and we're going to live on an island in the Hebrides.'

'That sounds exciting,' said Jennifer.

'It'll certainly be different!'

Jennifer looked at her doubtfully. 'Have you liked working here?'

Nurse Griffiths stood for a moment as if deep in thought.

'Dr Constable is charming and good to work for. Everything here is luxurious, as you can see, and the food is out of this world. But I'd be doing you a disservice if I didn't tell you the other side—only as I see it, of course. You might feel quite differently.'

'Of course I realise that, but I would like to know all you can tell me before I make up my mind.'

'Well—personally I don't really care for the type of patient we often get here. In an NHS hospital you do have some authority, but here—' Nurse Griffiths shook her head, 'here you're at their beck and call.'

Jennifer wrinkled her nose. 'That's not much fun.'

'No. And I do miss being on the wards. Private rooms mean much more work, and it's lonely. I

mean, there's a certain amount of fun and cama-
raderie on a ward, but there's none of that here.
But it's a matter of taste, some nurses prefer private
practice. Have you had any experience of it?'

Jennifer shook her head. 'No, I haven't, but I
know exactly what you mean. My problem is that
I've nothing else lined up and might not have for
ages. And as you say, Dr Constable is very kind,
and working under him should be a lot better than
in a hospital where they were all strangers.'

'Well, think it over. I shan't be leaving for
another two weeks.'

'I see. Is Dr Constable here? I'd like to see him
before I leave, if he can spare the time.'

'He's been called out. He hoped to be here when
you came, but he said would you give him a ring
when you've made up your mind. Oh,' Nurse
Griffiths said as an afterthought, 'his secretary
asked me to let her know when you were leaving.'

'That's Sarah—Miss Betts?'

'So you know her?'

'Only slightly. She's engaged to one of the
doctors at St Anselm's.'

'Is she?' Nurse Griffiths sounded surprised. 'I
wonder if she'll be leaving, then?'

Jennifer shook her head. 'I've no idea of their
plans.'

'I'll see what she wants,' Nurse Griffiths said,
picking up the phone. When she replaced the receiver she said, 'She's left some papers for Dr

Grant at the reception desk and wants you to take them to him, please.' She gave Jennifer a look that spoke volumes, and reminded her that if she came here to work Sarah would be a force to be reckoned with. Unless, of course, she left to get married. But that possibility did nothing to cheer Jennifer up.

Trust Sarah to expect her to deliver her mail to Roger without bothering to question whether she would be going to the hospital or straight home! She'd been intending to do the latter, but on seeing a bus for the hospital about to leave she hopped on it. It was a better alternative to spending the evening with Bernard and Aunt Marian. Her thoughts went longingly to the flatlet she had just seen; it would be just what she wanted.

Because it was visiting time the car park was full and she saw that Roger's car was in his parking space. With any luck she might see him. She went to his office and knocked on the door, but there was no answer, so she decided to leave the papers on his desk. To her surprise Roger was sitting at his desk, his head resting on his hands.

'What the hell do you want?' he barked, without turning around.

Jennifer stiffened. 'I'm sorry, but I've got some papers here for you from Sarah.'

'Oh—it's you. Forgive me.' He didn't look up.

When she put the papers on his desk she saw the lines on his face and his air of utter dejection.

'Is something wrong?' she asked softly.

He tried to speak, but no sound came. After a minute he said bleakly,

'It's Wendy.'

'I know—Rose told me she was showing signs of rejection, but with the increased anti-rejection drug this may just be a setback.' She knew that it was ludicrous that she, a nurse, was telling him this, but she longed to say something to comfort him.

He looked at her then, his eyes two dark pools of misery.

'We've lost her.' His voice broke.

The meaning of his words exploded in her head. 'Oh no!'

In a sudden fury he thumped his desk, making Jennifer jump.

'We just needed a suitable transplant in the beginning. Why in God's name don't people carry donor cards? Thousands of healthy organs which could save lives or greatly improve the quality of life, or enable a blind person to see, are wasted. Buried or cremated. Of no possible use to the person who's died.' Roger closed his eyes in despair.

'Well, I suppose it's something like making a will, a lot of people put that off in the mistaken belief that it makes death seem less likely,' Jennifer reminded him.

'I know, and I can understand that. But the relatives should give permission for the organs to be used.' He dredged the words up from somewhere deep down inside him.

'When people are bereaved it must be very difficult for them to think of anything other than their own sorrow,' Jennifer suggested.

Roger looked at her sadly. 'You're right, of course. But think of the waste. Why should a child like Wendy have to die when a kidney, of no possible use to the person who has died, might save her? They've got it right in France, where surgeons can take any organs they need without delay and without causing the relatives distress by having to ask their permission.'

'There are people who might have strong views on that,' Jennifer said.

Roger shook his head. 'If they would only think sensibly about it, how could they object? The organs are no good to the dead.'

'Maybe not. But people have a right to their own views.'

'Then heaven preserve me from people like that. Damnation!'

He sounded so desolate that she ached to comfort him, so much so that she barely thought of Wendy, the cause of his unhappiness. With loving intuition she knew that he would prefer to be alone to come to terms with his grief.

'I'll be going now, Roger,' she said softly.

'Good night,' he murmured.

'I've put the papers from Sarah over there,' she said, thinking that they might be urgent. But she guessed he wouldn't be dealing with them tonight.

CHAPTER TWELVE

ROGER sat at the large wooden desk in his office studying X-ray pictures and making diagnoses. Heather's arm had healed sufficiently for her to be sent home and in normal circumstances he would give that order, but he felt unhappy at exposing her to possible further physical injury. Clearly she didn't seem eager to leave the hospital. He stared thoughtfully at the poster on the wall in front of him which advised parents to have their children immunised against measles, diphtheria and whooping cough, but he didn't see it. He was seeing the pathetic child who appeared to be scared of men. He tapped his chin with his pen and frowned. The hospital, in common with others in all parts of the country, was having to cut expenditure. He shook his head regretfully. He couldn't justify keeping Heather here any longer when there was no medical reason to do so. He prepared to write his decision on her chart, paused for a moment, then completed it in his large scrawl before placing it on the pile of those he had dealt with.

He picked up the next chart but felt unable to concentrate on it. He ran his large fingers through his hair and sighed. It was a dark windy day and the windows rattled. He turned to see if they were properly closed as a cold draught crept in from somewhere, and through the glass he saw the trees bending and swaying to and fro, silhouetted against the pewter grey sky. He felt horribly depressed. Despite all his training which stressed that you must never become emotionally involved with a patient he still felt a deep sorrow at Wendy's death. It was such a waste. But it wasn't only that which was making him unhappy. There was Sarah and her ambition for him. She was probably right in wanting to see him get to the top of his profession, have status and a far higher salary. Many men would prize a woman who acted as a spur to them and who had such confidence in their ability. Harley Street. It could be all right, James was happy enough and there would be the additional bonus of holding clinics in NHS hospitals. But it wouldn't be the same as working on a ward and getting to know the patients, monitoring their day-to-day condition and treating them accordingly, which was the life he loved. But the biggest drawback to working in Harley Street was the fact that Sarah would have to finance him initially. She said it wasn't just him who would benefit, but both of them, and she preferred her husband to have a Harley Street practice. She had the money, so why not use it to enable him to make more?

That sounded reasonable enough, but all his life he had virtually pulled himself up by his shoelaces and he had no wish to change, nor did he believe it was in his nature to do so. They had fought over the idea like cat and dog—she, elegantly dignified, grey eyes hostile, tail waving and claws unsheathed ready to attack if he should go too far; he, large and noisy, barking and growling, dodging her out-stretched paw, knowing that he could silence her with one bite, but somehow not doing that.

Another thing that was like a weight on his heart was the knowledge that Jennifer was leaving St Anselm's. That shouldn't matter to him at all, since she was committed elsewhere. Indeed it would be easier when she had actually gone and there was no possibility of seeing the slim, fair-haired girl with the fascinating heart-shaped face and deep blue eyes. But how he would miss teasing her and watch-ing the embarrassed colour flooding her cheeks and chatting to her as if they'd known each other for years.

He shook his head impatiently and tried to con-centrate on his work, when his telephone rang. He was relieved at the interruption and pleased when his secretary told him that a Mrs Dickenson wanted to see him.

'Shall I ask her to make an appointment?' the disembodied voice asked.

'No, Pam, send her up, please.'

It would be one of the mothers, anxious about her child's treatment. Dickenson? Now which child would that be? He only knew them by their first names. He riffled through the pile of charts before him in vain. Every mother thought, quite naturally, that her own child was of primary importance and this one wouldn't take kindly to the fact that he didn't know who she was talking about. He would have to proceed carefully eliciting from her the information he needed.

He watched the woman as she entered the room and with a feeling of relief noted that she was more likely to be a grandmother than a mother, so the name could therefore be different.

He stood up and indicated the chair in front of his desk.

'Good morning, Mrs Dickenson, please sit down.'

He guessed she was in her late forties. She was tall and well built and dressed warmly against the chilly day in a fleecy-lined sheepskin coat over brown slacks. Untying a yellow and rust silk headsquare, she tucked it in her leather handbag, then ran her fingers through her short straight hair.

'You wanted to speak to me?' Roger's voice was quieter than usual.

She flicked him a quick glance. 'Yes, I'm only here for the day and it's good of you to see me without an appointment.'

This was getting them nowhere.

'And how can I help you?' he prompted.

She cleared her throat. 'I—I read an article

about you in a magazine,' she began.

Oh lord, she was probably a journalist anxious to write a follow-up to the article on him and to learn more about his past. She would want to probe his real feelings at having been abandoned as a baby, and that was the last thing he wanted to talk about today. So he did nothing to help her but continued to look down at his desk. She seemed to be hoping he would say something, but she would have to work hard to find out anything she wanted to know.

'And—and when I read it——' She stopped talking and twisted her hands together.

Roger felt a wave of irritation. She was making very heavy weather of the interview—was he so intimidating? He knew he could be, but Mrs Dickenson was no shy young girl, indeed she was herself a commanding figure. It was just that she was lacking in self-confidence. Possibly she was new to her job.

'Yes?' He knew he sounded abrupt, but he still had a lot of work to get through.

'This is dreadfully difficult,' she sighed unhappily.

He stifled a sigh and decided that after all it would be better to help her say what she wanted to say and get rid of her.

'So how can I help you if you won't tell me what it is you want to know?' He hated his brusque manner, but that was the way he was feeling.

She shook her head, her long brown ear-rings

dangling. 'I don't want to know anything, I want to tell you something.'

'Well, fire away.'

With a visible effort she said, 'When I read that article I realised I was reading about my own son.'

Roger's head shot up and he stared at her unbelievingly.

'Your *what*?' he demanded.

This was going to be difficult to deal with, but that article had made him vulnerable. Any slightly deranged woman could come forward claiming to be his mother. Possibly she had lost a child and saw in him a replacement.

'Tell me more,' he said guardedly.

She shook her head. 'You don't believe me, do you?'

'I've no reason to either believe or disbelieve you,' he replied.

'I had you in the ladies' cloakroom at Harrods and left you there in one of their carrier bags,' she told him in a low voice,

'You read that in the magazine, you know.' His voice was gentler now. 'Tell me about your son, the one you lost. Was it recently?'

'You still don't believe me,' she said angrily. 'I knew this was going to be difficult, but I had no idea it would be as bad as this.'

His eyes roamed over her. Could she be telling the truth? She had brown eyes, a large face and was a big woman with a clear voice, but were those

similarities enough to add up to such a close relationship? His mother! Did he want this woman to
be that?

'You must tell me more,' he said.

'I will, but please don't look at me in that hostile
way. I'm telling the truth,' she protested.

Roger lowered his head. 'Perhaps if you start at
the beginning?'

He groaned inwardly. Was he going to be treated
to a long rigmarole, a tissue of lies dramatised by
her?

She ran her tongue across her lips. 'The
beginning? Do you mean my own life as a child?
Because that's where it really starts.'

'Very well, start where you like, only——'
Roger flicked back his cuff and looked pointedly at
his watch.

'I understand,' the woman said in a flat voice.
'Your work is more important than hearing my
story, but I must tell you.'

'Of course. Then I suggest you get on with it.' He
was being curt, which was unlike him, but she was
dabbling in matters which affected him deeply.

She took a deep breath. 'My father—your grandfather—was the vicar of a parish in Oxfordshire.
He was a good man and—and his parishioners
thought the world of him. But he was one of these
people who believed there was good and evil but
had no time for the in-between. If someone in his
parish did something wrong he'd come down on

them heavily, they couldn't expect sympathy from him, they'd have to suffer the consequences of what they'd done. And strangely they all loved and respected him for that. In a way they knew where they stood.'

She paused, her eyes moving restlessly from side to side as she endeavoured to decide how best to continue.

'That doesn't sound a particularly Christian outlook,' Roger remarked.

'No, it wasn't. The Bishop tried to reason with him over his attitude, but he was a self-willed man and I don't think anyone could have changed him. The majority of his parishioners didn't want him to be different.'

Self-willed? He himself had been called that on many occasions.

Mrs Dickenson picked up her handbag and took from it some photographs which she sorted through, then passed one of them to Roger.

'That's your grandfather,' she said.

He held it between his long fingers and saw a big man with an untidy beard and hair which was thick and long. His dark eyes beneath straight brows had a stern expression, as if the photographer had committed some unforgivable sin. He had a strong straight nose and a mouth which Roger realised was shaped like his own, turning slightly down at the corners. As he continued to stare down at it she said,

'Can you see there's a strong resemblance?'

He looked up at her with new interest. If the man in the photograph was indeed his grandfather then this was his mother. He had a tremendous urge to know more.

He nodded and waited for her to continue.

'As you can imagine, Mother and I had to be, like Caesar's wife, beyond reproach. He even had me christened Angel, but I managed to be called Angela at school. Poor Mother was so timid she never ventured an opinion in case it differed from his.' She rested her chin on her hand.

'When I look back I can see our vicarage as a large, cold house with Father as an avenging angel —or a saint. If something angered him his voice bellowed through the house, condemning everything and everybody. But when he was pleased he would be loving and gentle and sometimes amusing.' She fiddled with the clasp of her handbag. 'It wasn't an easy atmosphere to be brought up in—at least I didn't find it so. I was always either too happy or too sad according to his moods.'

The sudden ring of the telephone made them both start. Roger picked it up and listened.

'I'm sorry, I can't be disturbed. I'll let you know when I'm free.' He replaced the receiver and prompted her to continue.

'You were saying——'

'When I reached my teens he became even more strict. Understandably, I suppose, for a man like that. It wouldn't do for the Reverend Roger Bates to have a wayward daughter.'

She glanced at the other photographs which she had put on the desk and picking one up she looked at it before passing it across to Roger.

'A family group. Mother, Father and me.'

Roger took it eagerly. Angela Dickenson had been an athletic-looking girl, not pretty but with an attractive smile. Was she his mother? He waited as if he expected his heart to register some emotion, but it didn't. He turned his gaze on to the older woman, who had a sad, sweet smile and wore her hair brushed smoothly into a bun. Her dress was modest with a high neck and long sleeves. He looked again at the young girl and saw that she was dressed similarly. The vicar towered above them both, a watch-chain stretched across his waistcoat plainly visible. This was his picture, his wife and daughter mere appendages. That was how it looked to Roger.

'Is he still alive—your father?' he asked.

'No, he died several years ago, disapproving of me even on his deathbed. Mother died soon afterwards, which was a shame. She could have enjoyed her freedom, but I think she'd never learned how to.'

'Your father sounds a typical Victorian master of the house, but that was before his time.' Roger wondered whether she was exaggerating.

Mrs Dickenson nodded slowly. 'He really was

the kind of Victorian father you read about in books. In his case it was because he was so religious. I wasn't allowed to dance—not even in the Church Hall. He didn't approve of dances being held there, but he was overruled on that occasion by the Church Council. As for alcohol! That was devil's brew, and people who touched it were heading straight for Hell.'

'That sounds a very bleak life for a young lady. How did you get your amusement?' asked Roger, feeling sorry for the woman in front of him.

She gave a wry smile. 'At prayer meetings and choir practice.'

'I see.'

Her description of life at the vicarage seemed to preclude any possibility of her having a relationship with a man, which she clearly must have done if she was indeed his mother.

'Father always wanted me to become a teacher. I was never asked how I felt about that, and the truth was that I would have loathed it,' she said vehemently.

'*Would* have? So you did escape his tyranny that time?'

She gave a small mischievous smile. 'I failed the exams.'

Roger mentally congratulated her on that action, it was something he would have done himself.

'So what was his second choice for you? A lady's maid?' he smiled.

She laughed. 'No doubt it would have been if there were such things in those days. I'm not all that old. When I had you I was seventeen.'

He glanced down at the family group again. She was about that age in it, and that was how she would have looked. Poor little Angel!

'It was then that I had my first real break. I wasn't very good at anything other than art, and that appealed to me. My art teacher told my parents that I had a gift and should be encouraged to use it, it was a God-given gift. To tell the truth I thought she was wasting her breath, my father would never allow me to do that. Moreover, I knew she was exaggerating when she said I had a gift. I think she probably guessed more about my father's tyranny that she let on.'

'So he agreed that you should do that?'

'Yes. I passed the exam to get to the art college. All the time he inspected my work, and if he'd come across any nude figures I'd have been out of there like a shot.'

There was a slight look of amusement in Roger's eyes. 'Did you draw any?'

'Of course—it was a part of the course. But I had the sense to leave them at college.'

He was eager now to hear the rest of her story, but he didn't want to hurry her in case he missed something important.

'We had evening classes as well as day classes. You know, if someone is too strict it makes you deceitful. At times my friends and I used to skip the evening ones and go into the town, and I felt so free! It was the first time I was able to live like other girls my age.'

'I'm glad. And what sensible person could blame you?' said Roger, staring down at the picture of the self-righteous clergyman.

'I know. But you see, I was so inexperienced that when I had my first sherry it transported me to another world, made me feel I was the life and soul of the party. After a second one I felt like a bird who'd escaped from its cage. I was seeing and hearing things that were all new to me.'

Roger gave a nod of understanding. At last she must be coming to that part he wanted to hear, the identity of his father. And yet—was he some man she had met in a pub who had taken her against her will? Was he, therefore, liable to inherit his father's trait? He had an urge to stop her telling him anything more, but his curiosity was too great.

'We met boys—that was nothing new to the other girls, but to me they seemed like a strange, unknown breed of animals. I had no idea how to flirt until after I'd had a couple of drinks, and then I was completely uninhibited.' Mrs Dickenson ran her fingers through her hair again in a gesture he recognised as his own. 'Mostly the boys were from the university and out for fun, which I suppose they needed after all that studying.'

Roger had a sudden memory of some of the

students who boasted about the local girls they had picked up, when he was at university, and he felt a surge of indignant protection for that young girl she had been describing. She would have been out of her depth.

'They didn't take much notice of me, they were more interested in the other girls, and I felt left out. Then one night there was another student, one I hadn't seen before. He was tall and fair and muscular. He'd been rowing for his college that day. The others had paired off and that just left him and me. I liked him a lot, he was so different from the others, kind and gentle and not at all brash. After university he wanted to go to medical school —that's something you've inherited from him. Well, you've probably guessed that I fell hopelessly in love with him. I was young, he was my first love and so completely different from the only other man I knew well—my father—that I felt I would happily die for him.' She looked at Roger with raised eyebrows. 'What a thing young love is— nothing later in life is quite so strong.' She took a handkerchief from her pocket and dabbed her nose.

'There's really no need for me to tell you what happened next, but on my side it was love. He was so handsome, with smooth skin and classical fea- tures and a superb body. He made me feel large and clumsy and I couldn't see what he saw in me at all. It was to be his last year at university and they held a party in his rooms. I smuggled out a childish party dress from home and hid it in my holdall under my drawing things.' There was a distant look in her eyes. 'We lay in each other's arms and——' She suddenly stopped talking and looked startled. 'I'm sorry, I'm embarrassing you. I was forgetting——'

Roger shook his head. 'Please go on. Although I'm your son I'm also a doctor and trained to listen.'

'I'm sure you're an excellent one. I often wonder whether—he was able to qualify. I do hope so.'

Roger waited for her to continue. Her voice was low and reluctant.

'By the time I knew that I was pregnant he'd gone to a medical school in London.'

'You could have contacted him,' Roger said more sharply than he knew.

'I know. But I'd have died first, because the last thing I wanted to do was to ruin his career or embarrass him. You see, although I was in love with him I knew he didn't feel the same about me. I was dull and dowdy.'

'All the same, you should have told him, you shouldn't have had to face it on your own. Your father? How did he take it?'

Mrs Dickinson laughed then, a harsh, unamused laugh. 'If I'd told him, if he'd guessed, I'd have been out in the street right away, and that's a fact.'

Roger pressed his fingers together. 'I doubt if you're right about that. Once he'd got over the shock and his anger he'd have come round.'

She shook her head. 'You didn't know him. When at last I got married he disapproved because my husband was an artist, and in his opinion that wasn't a proper job. But eventually he accepted him reluctantly.'

'And it's lasted—your marriage?'

'No. Sean could never settle down. He was a loner and preferred to live on his own.'

Roger glanced at her expensive clothes. She seemed to be well provided for. Maybe she was a successful artist herself. Before he could ask her she said,

'To prove how impossible it would have been to tell Father about you—when Sean and I got divorced, and it was quite an amicable parting, Father never spoke to me again. I went to visit him when he was dying and I'll never forget the look of accusation and—hatred—in his eyes.'

Roger felt as if a cold hand had touched his heart. 'And you say I resemble him? That's a frightening thought.'

She gave a dismissive gesture. 'I'm telling you that side of him, the side that made me do what I did. Other people thought he was a wonderfully kind man, and in some ways he was. He was different with Mother and me because I suppose he felt he and his family must be a good example to his parishioners. You mustn't think of him as an evil man, because he wasn't. If I'd been the sort of girl he thought I was, everything would have been all right.'

Roger thought for a moment. 'Did your mother know you were pregnant?'

'Oh no! She would have hated to have to lie to him. I don't think she could have done, anyway.'

'So what did you do?'

'Fortunately I was still at art school, where we all dressed in zany clothes. I wore smocks and voluminous skirts and nobody guessed. Fortunately Father didn't disapprove of my dress, because I was well covered up.'

'How did you come to have me in Harrods?' queried Roger.

'I'd wondered what to do. When I knew you were about due I told Mother and Father I'd been invited to spend a few days with a friend, for half-term. I felt really guilty when they believed me. Actually I went to London and stayed at the YWCA. I still had no idea what would happen or where, or how I would cope. As it happened it was all very quick and straightforward. You know the rest.'

He shook his head despairingly. 'Didn't you know you should have had medical attention?'

'Not really. I bought some towels in Harrods and I used one for you and one for myself. I'd also bought a writing pad, and I wrote a note and pinned it to the towel saying I wanted you to be called Roger. Did they ever show that to you?'

'Yes. I still have it. Why did you call me Roger?'

A glint came into her eyes. 'It was my father's name, and it gave me a kind of unchristian pleasure to call you after him. I felt I had to tell you all this when I read that article and discovered where you were—I rang up about that, beforehand I had no idea of your name, you see. You've done marvels, Roger.' She shrugged sadly. 'You probably did better without me.'

Roger had a sudden memory of Mary Jenks, his housemother, who had been so kind and loving and caring. He couldn't transfer his affection to someone he had only just met, it would be too disloyal. He made no reply.

Angela Dickinson looked hurt. 'I didn't get away scot free, you know.'

He looked at her with warmth and compassion. 'I'm quite certain you didn't. It was a dreadful ordeal. And I have you to thank for my life.'

'What I meant was that because I didn't see a doctor after you were born I'm unable to have any more children,' she explained.

'I'm sorry. Did you want to have some?' he asked gently.

'My husband would have liked a family,' she said.

'Your husband? But——'

'I married again, and we're very happy.' She looked at him warily. 'I don't want him to know about you, ever. It would alter everything.'

'You don't think he would understand?'

'I don't want him to know,' she said firmly.

'Does that mean—that you'd rather not keep in touch?' Roger asked.

She wrung her hands together and stared at the floor. 'It would be best. I lost my right to you all those years ago. I only came here today because I felt you had the right to know who you were. I felt so sad when I read that article.' She stood up and began putting on her gloves. 'I must be going now, I didn't mean to take up so much of your time, I had no idea it would take so long.' She gave a small smile. 'I'm afraid I've disrupted the work of the hospital.'

'That's all right, it can function very well without me for once. Have you far to go?'

'To Devon. I'll go down on the night train.'

He joined her beside the door. 'Thank you for coming,' he said. 'Naturally I've always wondered about my parents, and I'm very glad to have met you. It's good to know that you're somebody I can be proud of. About my father—what was his name?'

She frowned. 'I promised myself I would never tell anybody.'

He looked at her steadily and said quietly, 'I would like you to tell me, please. I think I have the right to know.'

She gave a slight shrug. 'Being in the medical world it's possible that you might meet, but I want you to promise me you'll never mention me to him.

I know it's unlikely, but I wouldn't want to hurt him.'

'You can rely on me,' he assured her.

'His friends called him Copper. His name was James Constable.'

For a moment Roger felt transfixed, unable to act naturally. Then he pulled himself together.

'Thank you,' he said, and held out his hand.

His mother looked at it for a moment, then raised her eyes to his.

'You don't feel inclined to kiss me goodbye, I suppose?' she asked wistfully.

He reached out and took her in his arms, and as he did so he felt a wave of pity and affection. How she must have suffered, and no doubt still did. How different her life would have been if her father had not been such a hard man.

'Goodbye, Mother,' he said softly. 'Thank you, and keep happy.'

She squeezed his hand, then hastily brushed tears from her eyes before going out into the corridor.

Roger leaned against the closed door, his mind in turmoil. In the last hour he had learned more about himself than he had ever dreamed he would. Now he felt as if he were a plant which had thrived for many years and was now uprooted and trans-planted. His poor mother—what a rotten life she had had, but she had come through and seemed to be happy now. James! He was not yet able to fully take that in. It was strange they had always been so fond of one another, and only recently James had suggested that they go into partnership. If his mother had married James and they had been a family, he wouldn't be different from what he was now. He would have been a doctor for sure. However, he wouldn't have had the experience of being brought up in an institution, and that had been good for him. For there he was one of very many children, no more and no less important than any of the others. There were no expensive toys or presents and anything they received—for the housemother was very kind—had to be shared.

As for James—it was probably better for him that he hadn't known, for he would have undoubtedly married Angela when he knew she was pregnant, although, as she admitted, he didn't love her. All in all things had worked out all right for the three of them, almost as if their futures had been predestined.

CHAPTER THIRTEEN

Two THINGS happened to Jennifer the following week. The first, which was expected, was the arrival of the letter she had been dreading, telling her that her temporary post at St Anselm's was at an end on the first Saturday in February. The second was totally unexpected. Bernard invited her to the theatre. Neither event pleased her and the second one puzzled her, since Bernard was not one to squander his money. Maybe it was a show he particularly wanted to see, but when she checked the posters it was a new play with an unknown cast. If for some reason he wanted to see it, why invite her and so have the double expense? Why not go alone?

'Why am I so honoured?' she asked him.

He smoothed his silky moustache lovingly. One of these days the damn thing will fall off, and a good job too, Jennifer thought nastily.

'Because I like to treat my girl sometimes, that's why,' he said.

She felt cornered. She didn't want to go with him yet she didn't want to disappoint him.

'Which night did you have in mind?' she asked cautiously.

'Why, tonight,' he said with his air of surprise.

With a sense of relief she said, 'Oh, I'm sorry, but I promised to work a couple of hours for Sister tonight.' Then seeing the light fade from his eyes she added weakly, 'I could manage tomorrow night.'

'That's no good,' he said furiously. 'Blast! The tickets are for tonight.'

'You've already got them?'

'Yes. You don't usually work on Thursday nights. You're not having me on, are you?'

'No, it's the truth. But you can change the tickets. Ring up the box office.'

He looked sulky. 'I can't do that, they're complimentary tickets—one of my pupils gave them to me.'

Jennifer felt sorry for him. He had two tickets and nobody to accompany him, because his mother didn't like going out at night. Suddenly she thought of Debbie.

'Why don't you ask Debbie? You know, you met her at the party. She's on duty, why not give her a ring?'

Bernard came back from the phone looking so smug that she was almost sorry she'd suggested it.

'She jumped at the chance.' He tapped his nose. 'Between you and me, she sounded a bit smitten.'

'Smitten? What do you mean?'

'With me, old girl. You may live to regret this

move, you know.' He gave her bottom a friendly slap in passing.

Jennifer pressed her lips together and stared at the ceiling, thinking longingly of the flat in Harley Street. She wished Debbie and Bernard could fall in love, but she doubted it. Debbie thought Bernard was attractive, but Jennifer had the feeling that Bernard either couldn't or wouldn't allow himself to fall in love with a girl who was available. He could pretend interest in someone like Sarah Betts who was out of his reach, but she had a strong suspicion that when it came to the crunch he would be away like a frightened rabbit.

When she had told Bernard she was working tonight it had been the truth, and now she sat in the staff room during her break sipping coffee and staring into space, trying to decide her future, for time was running out and she still hadn't made up her mind. Her thoughts went to and fro. They had the best of everything at the clinic, nobody could be nicer to work for than Dr Constable, she would have a higher salary and, best of all, her own flat. On the other hand, the prospect of dealing with patients privately and having no ward duties was depressing, added to which there was Nurse Griffiths' warning about the patients' attitude to the nurses. And worst of all was the fact that Sarah worked there, and she had to admit that she didn't like her. And at times she was almost bound to see her with Roger. It would be bad enough not working with him, without seeing him in those circumstances.

Roger, coming into the room, saw her sitting there and his heart lifted. Then he saw her pensive, dispirited air and felt a longing to protect her from anything that would make her sad. For he knew now that she was the girl he wanted in his home, his bed, his life. With a sudden ache in his loins he longed for her to have his children. He had never felt that way about Sarah, who had attracted him initially because of her looks and style and he was proud to be seen with her. The fact that she didn't want to have children was an added bonus, as he had had doubts about his unknown parentage. Now his mother had done more than satisfy his curiosity on that score, for she had made it possible for him to have a family without those doubts. But what was the use when the girl he loved was committed to another man?

Jennifer glanced up and, seeing him, waved to him. He returned the gesture and went across to join her.

'You're looking very worried about something,' he remarked, pulling out a chair beside her. 'What's the trouble?'

Jennifer shrugged. 'I'm thinking about my future because I've had my marching orders. I can't decide where to go next.'

So the time had come, and the hospital would seem empty without her.

'Have you had any offers?' he asked.

'Just one,' she said, toying with her spoon.

'And how many do you want?'

'I suppose in my heart I don't want to leave here, so nowhere would seem very tempting,' she said sadly.

He nodded. 'So what's the offer?'

'It's at Dr Constable's London clinic,' she told him, and his heart missed a beat. 'It's a lovely place, but I'd miss working here with the children and ——' She had been going to say, 'And with you'. But she stopped in time.

Roger's eyes looked deeply into hers. 'And?' he prompted.

'And—and I'm not sure that I'd like private practice,' she said instead.

'I don't think you would either,' he agreed.

She looked at him accusingly. 'But that's what you're going to do, and quite frankly I'm amazed. I shouldn't have thought you'd have liked it either.'

'Now how the devil did that leak out?' he asked angrily. 'It's hopeless to keep anything secret in a hospital!'

'You mustn't blame the hospital, nobody has mentioned it here. It was Sarah who told me.'

'Then Sarah's got it wrong, as well she knows. She's been pushing for it because she's ambitious for me and can't understand me preferring NHS work, it's too down-market. She'd like to see my name on a brass plate in Harley Street, and me togged up in an immaculate suit complete with buttonhole.' He gave an unamused chuckle. 'As I told her, it's no use trying to make a silk purse out of a sow's ear.'

Jennifer couldn't imagine either of them giving in when they had an argument. 'So who won?' she asked.

'We had a blazing row. I won, noise-wise, but she won by not losing her temper. But it made us both realise for sure something we'd suspected for some time, that we were totally unsuited to each other.'

Jennifer put her hand on his arm. 'I'm sorry it didn't work out.'

His eyes softened. 'There's no need to be. I've known for some time that I didn't love Sarah. And her love for me was contained in what she thought she could make of me. She should have realised that I'd made myself how I want to be.'

Jennifer gave a relieved sigh. 'So you won't be leaving here—the children would have missed you dreadfully if you had, you'd have been a great loss to the hospital.'

He smiled. 'Such flattery! So what about this Harley Street job? Are you going to accept it?'

She shook her head. 'I honestly can't make up my mind,' she confessed.

'What does your boy-friend have to say about it?'

'My boy-friend?' Her cheeks flamed.

'Yes—Bernard. Surely you've discussed it with him?'

Jennifer stared down at the table. There was no reason now that she was leaving for her not to tell him the truth. 'Bernard was never my boy-friend. I—I pretended he was for reasons of my own. Actually he's my cousin, and I'm living with my aunt and him.' She looked up at Roger earnestly. 'The thought of moving from there and having a flat of my own in London is almost enough to make me take the job whether I'd like it or not.' She glanced at her watch and started to get up from the table.

Roger put his hand over hers to detain her. She was free, and suddenly the world seemed to him a brighter place.

'Don't go,' he said.

'I must. I'm standing in for Rose and I must get back to the ward.'

'I don't mean now. I'm talking about the future.'

'You mean don't go to the clinic?'

'I mean don't go anywhere.'

He was infuriating! she thought.

'What's the use of saying that?' she exclaimed. 'You know perfectly well I've got to leave. Don't you think I'd stay here if I could?'

Roger drew his chair closer and she was ecstatically conscious of his nearness.

'I love you, Jennifer,' he said quietly.

Or had she imagined it? Her head shot up.

'Wh-what did you say?' she stammered.

'I said I love you. If I'd had to fashion a girl who

was the girl of my dreams I'd have made you.' He smiled at her tenderly.

She looked up at his rugged face, his gentle eyes that seemed to caress her, and love and happiness flooded through her.

'And I've loved you since I first met you, but——'

'You always seemed to keep me at a distance. If it wasn't because of Bernard, then why was it?' he asked, holding her hand tightly.

'Because there was Sarah, and I hated you trying to get too friendly with me because I know what men are and I don't trust them.'

His thoughts went to his mother. 'And quite right too,' he agreed, then added with a smile, 'But you can trust me, I promise you. Both Sarah and I had already begun to have doubts about our relationship before you came along. Tell me, did you really fall in love with me from the start?'

She nodded. 'How could I help it?'

'Then prove it,' he said, lifting her face to his.

His kiss was unbelievable bliss, and Jennifer could happily have stayed like that for ever. But at last Roger drew away and said as excitedly as a small boy discussing the imminent arrival of Santa Claus,

'We'll have a big wedding and invite all the staff. I want them all to know that I'm the luckiest guy in the world. Tell me, how soon can we make it?'

Her heart lurched sickeningly. A wedding! As if in a nightmare she saw again the church, the bridesmaids and her father's embarrassment. She knew her wedding dress was still hanging in her wardrobe, as her mother hadn't wanted to dispose of it. But Jennifer knew that she could never wear it, nor any other.

'Married? Oh, I can't marry you,' she said frantically, and saw the happiness drain from his face.

'You can't marry me? What do you mean? You said you loved me.'

'I do, Roger, I really do. But we don't need to get married. Can't we just live together?'

His voice was harsh with anger and disappointment. 'No, we can't. If you don't want to marry me then you have the right to refuse. Obviously I don't know you as well as I thought I did. I had no idea you were one of these modern girls who'll live with a man and have his children but have the stupid idea that if she marries him she loses her independence. I don't want a girl like that. Maybe I'm old-fashioned, maybe it's because of my background, but I'll only settle for marriage. I want a wife who'll be proud to have children who will bear my name. I know it's a made-up name, but I'm proud of it, and I want to feel proud of my family.' His usually gentle eyes were hostile as he stared down at her.

Jennifer's eyes stung with tears. 'It isn't that I don't want to be married to you, it's—just that I couldn't face the wedding,' she said brokenly.

Roger put an arm around her shoulders. 'That's

just nerves, my dear. Most girls love a wedding where they can dress up and have all the trimmings and celebrations. I should have thought you would have enjoyed that, and you'd make a beautiful bride.' He looked at her questioningly. 'Why don't you want that?'

She covered her face with her hands. She couldn't tell him what had happened, it was too shaming.

He gently removed her hands and held them in his. 'Tell me,' he insisted.

'I—I can't,' she protested.

'I want you to tell me, Jennifer,' he said firmly.

She knew he would eventually get his way and steeled herself to speak. Slowly, hesitatingly, hating every moment, she described to him that dreadful day, not wanting his pity—she had had too much of that from friends and relations. When at last she had finished telling him, his eyes blazed.

'The rotten bastard!' he growled. Then, after a moment's thought, he said, 'Do you still love him?'

'Love Simon?' She shook her head. 'For some time afterwards I thought I did—although I hated him too. Then, when I went home at Christmas, I met him accidentally in the street, and suddenly I knew without any doubt that I'd never really loved him and I felt a wonderful feeling of release. By then, you see, I'd met you,' she said shyly. 'And although I knew I mustn't love you, because of

Sarah, I couldn't help myself. That's why I kept you at a distance.'

'But love and trust must go together, and you mustn't condemn all men because of the actions of one. You say you love me and I hope you trust me too.'

'I do—it's not that. It's the wedding ceremony I can't face. Can't you understand that?' Her eyes filled with tears.

Roger cupped her face in his hands and wiped away a trickling tear with his finger.

'This should be the happiest of occasions, Jennifer, not a time for tears. If you feel so strongly about it we won't have that big wedding, we'll have a quiet one—no staff, just a few friends and relations, and I'd like to invite the Constables,' he said.

Jennifer longed to agree, but she knew she couldn't. She shook her head.

'My parents, and my friends—they'd all be remembering. And I'd be remembering too. It was too awful!'

'You poor darling, how you must have suffered. I didn't realise. I tell you what we'll do. We'll have a secret wedding, just the two of us, either in church or at a register office, whichever you prefer. How would that be?'

Her eyes shone like stars. 'Oh, Roger, I do love you! So it would be just the two of us?'

'Just the two of us,' he promised.

He held her so closely and kissed her so

passionately that by the time he had released her she was breathless.

From the doorway came the sound of clapping and cheering. They looked around and saw applauding colleagues.

'Encore,' they cried. 'Encore!'

But Roger needed no such encouragement to take her in his arms again.

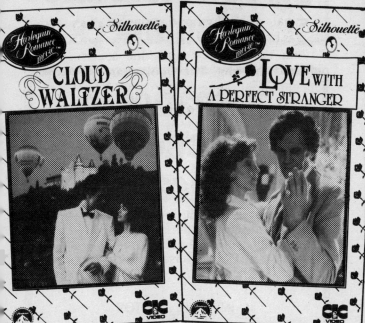

NOW ON VIDEO

Two great Romances available on video . . .

from leading video retailers for just **£9·99**

R.R.P.

The love you find in Dreams.

from Autumn 1987

Doctor Nurse Romances

Romance in modern medical life

Read more about the lives and loves of doctors and nurses in the fascinatingly different backgrounds of contemporary medicine. These are the three Doctor Nurse romances to look out for next month.

INVISIBLE DOCTOR
Holly North

VALENTINES FOR NURSE CLEO
Lilian Darcy

NURSE ON THE MOVE
Frances Crowne

Buy them from your usual paperback stockist, or write to: Mills & Boon Reader Service, P.O. Box 236, Thornton Rd, Croydon, Surrey CR9 3RU, England. Readers in Southern Africa — write to: Independent Book Services Pty, Postbag X3010, Randburg, 2125, S. Africa.

Mills & Boon
the rose of romance